The Gates Keeper

I0563716

Andrea Johnson

Andrea Johnson Books Publishing

Other titles by Andrea Johnson

Blood of my Blood

The Embryos

Remember the Promise

Awaken the Promise

The King of Credence

eBooks by Andrea Johnson

His Nuclear Requiem

Voices of Tear Drops

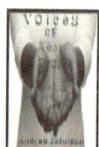

Behind the Forest

What They Don't Know

Her Mask

Vantanka

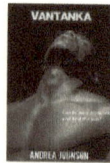

Visit Andrea's website for more of her upcoming books!

www.Andreajohnsonbooks.com

The Gates Keeper

Cover art designed by Andrea Johnson Books Publishing.

First published by Andrea Johnson Books Publishing. 10/11/2019

6565 N. MacArthur Blvd, Suite 225 Dallas, TX. 75039
www.Ajbpublishing.com

This is a work of fiction. Names, characters, places and incidents either are a product of the author's imagination, or used fictitiously. Any resemblance to actual persons, living or dead, events or locales, is entirely coincidental.

ISBN:13-978-0-578-59392-0

To my forever and a day. Not even the winds of change could ever keep us apart.

Prologue

Thousands of years ago, in a time when the planet was nothing but a platform for creatures that have been long extinct, a powerful species ruled the third world, known as earth.

They were known by many names, but the most common was called, Carpathians. A highly evolved version of the vampire. They were the keepers of the order. Extremely powerful beings that lived and cohabited with the large creatures of the earth.

But then, mankind was discovered. A lower, primitive species that roamed the mountains and the caves. The Carpathians saw that these humans were nothing but prey, to everything else that walked and lived. Including their own lustful temptation to feast on a different kind of sustenance. Living human blood. Some Carpathians began to hunt the humans. Enjoying the thrill and ecstasy received from taking their lives. But the others sought to protect these men and women that were helpless against them.

A division was created. The Carpathians that wanted to kill, became the vampire. A dark and insidious predator that was ten times deadlier than their counterparts. The others were known as the Protectors. Pure blood Carpathians that resisted and fought for the weaker species of man.

But the dividing of the powerful beings came at a deadly price. The more of their kind that turned to vampire, the weaker the Carpathian beings became.

Their leader, a strong and powerful ancient Carpathian, named Loron, made a grave sacrifice and a decision that would change the fate of their kind forever.

Seeing that their numbers grew smaller, Loron ordered his queen, Besilia, to take all the remaining Carpathian females, and go underground. Each female would be impregnated, and take the seed with them deep beneath the earth. If it were a male, they were to be raised to mate with chosen females, then sent above ground. However, the women were to stay beneath the earth, secluded in the tunnels designed to shelter them from harm.

But after centuries had passed, and the Carpathian males no longer remained on earth, males were no longer reproduced. Only females were born to the last of the remaining seeds.

It was queen Besilia that made the final decision, as she lay dying, that would save the female Carpathian species.

She handed a key to her most trusted aide. And made a declaration that was binding.

"Choose one special female that will protect this key. She must be vigilant, and resilient. She will need to go above ground and find a human male that possesses a good soul. This man will be chosen to help recreate our people. He and one female will reproduce. Choose a unique one from among us, and let her bring him here."

The queen stared at her lovely young aide who had been by her side for over a hundred years. The dying light in the queen's normally beautiful crystal eyes, filled with heat as she forced out her last words.

"However, if she cannot find a man with a good soul, let her destroy the ones who have destroyed us. Let her annihilate them all."

Queen Besilia died with those last words, a proclamation of hope and doom. Making a bitter and final attempt to save the last of her kind. She blamed mankind; you see. They were the ones whom her beloved king had chosen to protect. But instead, the humans had grown powerful in their numbers over the centuries, and hunted them. Growing wiser and more cunning over time, they had discovered their weaknesses. The humans had killed all remaining Carpathians, and vampires on the earth.

And so Besilia had forged the key. A key that would bring change, or death.

The search had begun. But for centuries, the underground lair of the Carpathian females grew large with tortured human male prisoners, but smaller in their own numbers. Each holder of the key would be tasked to go above ground and bring back a human male. But none but dark souls entered, and were ultimately tortured to death. And now, as the key is placed into the hands of one of the last remaining Carpathian females, Cassandra Martin, she will stop at nothing to save her people. Even if it means capturing every last human male on earth, and bringing him into the gate............

Chapter One

Sussex State Prison, (Death Row) Waverly, VA 2019

The men were silent as they were led onto the waiting bus. Today was not a day for words. All things had been said. All pleas if necessary, had been made. This was a time of finality and conclusion. And there was not a single man present, even the attending guards, that felt the need for idle speech.

Drago Brown kept his head lowered as he stepped onto the bus. The chains held his arms in front of him, and at his feet, and connected him to a man who shared the same fate as he did. Each of them paired together and bound in chains, like two halves of a split apple. Sliced, and ready to be served.

Drago silently walked over to the third section of seats on the bus, where his partner had led them. He took the row seat as the man to his right had chosen the window. Just as Drago had known he would. The entire process was one that was designed to mentally drain you, and terrorize any last vestige of hope from your mind. This was it. Once you were on this bus, you were headed to what the inmates called 'The dungeon.' Death row, to many of them, was the easy part. But going on that bus, and taking that final trip. That was the end of all things. And you were never coming back.

Drago sat as the bus began to move. He kept his eyes in front of him, staring at the back of the seat that faced him, and the fence that separated the guards from the prisoners. His face was a mask of stone. Like pieces of granite formed together not quite perfectly.

Drago was a tall man, but not overly stocky and large like the others. His build was more athletic, and sleek. As if he was designed for the outdoors, and mountain climbing. His skin was a smooth chocolate brown, and gave way to a face that was not handsome in the classic sense. But rough and distinguished. His full black beard had grown out over his face, giving him the look of a hardened miner, under thick strong lips that almost never smiled. His eyebrows were a dark brown, and thick as well. They covered the most unusual pupils, a soft topaz mixed with hazel green. An oddity that held most women captive in his gaze, and caused fear to race down men's spine.

He never had a problem with the ladies. As his body was perfectly toned and fit, even before he entered into prison. And it served him well in protecting himself, in a place where men normally were not known to survive the full term, of death row.

Drago closed his eyes as the familiar rage began to surface within him. The years he'd been locked up within the prison system, and the people who had strategically arranged to set him up, so he would end up there. Alone. Destitute. And hopeless.

All for what? The price he had paid was far too high for what they had done to him. And Drago had no intention of giving his life for something that should never have happened.

He opened his eyes and turned his gaze towards the window. His partner, an overweight balding Caucasian man, had his head down, and was oblivious to Drago's sudden interest in his surroundings. The trip would not be a long one. It was only a thirty five minute ride to the Greenville Correctional Center, in Jarratt Virginia. And Bailys

Pond was not far from that, but it wasn't on the path they were taking.

Drago had a topographic memory. It was one of his talents he'd been born with, among many others. Every moment of his carefully thought out plan had to be carried out to the letter, if there were any chance of it working.

It had to be executed at the precise moment.

Staring hard out the window, Drago counted the different landmarks he'd memorized in is mind. When he got to fifty, he knew it was time.

Glancing quickly to the front, he made certain the first guard was facing straight ahead. He was sitting in the first row, two seats in front of them, his attention focused on the road. The only other guard was the driver, protected by the iron fence that separated them.

He would only have a space of five minutes to do what was needed, but if done correctly, it was more than enough time.

Going into stealth mode, Drago made a lightning flash move with his elbow, and swiftly knocked his partner out cold. The loud rumbling of the bus covered the shocked grunt the man made, as his head was slammed into the back of the seat with brutal force. The impact was not designed to kill him, as Drago knew the guard would check for a pulse. But it helped to give him the freedom he needed to carry out his next move.

Acting fast now, Drago kept his eyes glued to the front, constantly watching the guard and driver. He moved his hands between his legs, and felt along the bottom front seam of the seat. The chains that bound him to his partner were the ones joined at the feet. Which left his imprisoned hands free within a few inches of themselves.

His heartbeat accelerated, Drago pressed his fingers carefully along the seat, looking for the opening he'd placed there, only five hours ago.

A plan that he had conjured and constructed for the past four years of his five year death row sentence.

Using his skills and the connection he'd formed with one of the guards who served on night watch, Drago was able to procure the chemicals needed to create sulfuric acid. Carefully putting together the substance that would enact his plan. He knew he would never be able to get it out of the building without detection. And he couldn't trust the guard to know exactly how to hide the chemical within the bus. And so, he had to do it himself. Which was far from easy. It was damn near impossible. Death row inmates were guarded round the clock. Sealed within solitary confinement, and not allowed anything that would cover up walls, windows, or the floors. So digging out from the walls was definitely out.

Drago knew he had to escape to do the deed, but once out, he would not attempt to leave the grounds. At least not that way. Not only would a man hunt immediately ensue, he would have to travel on foot for at least five miles. In which helicopters and police would have him surrounded.

Using the aide of the night watchman, Drago had secured the key to the outer gates, and was able to temporarily shut down the power to the outside lights. There was a backup generator, that kicked in within three minutes, so timing was of the essence.

He knew the bus would be waiting and sitting in the parking lot, because of the early start the guards would make in getting the inmates to the correctional center. He knew the exact location, and that it would be unattended. After all, there was no chance of escape on foot, so why bother for extra security? But a smart man always left room for error. And Drago didn't get this far by being stupid.

Never trusting anyone entirely, Drago added extra insurance to ensure the guard's cooperation. A double-cross at the end was always possible, as he'd learned from his experiences that landed him into the prison. And so having a little something over the guard always helped. If anything were to happen to Drago, the guard would lose everything. As Drago had manipulated the security tapes to catch him and another prisoner having sex within the showers. He'd informed the guard that he'd mailed a copy of the tape to someone. So if he died, the tape would be released.

The rest was easy. The guard ensured he would find the bus vacant, and the timeframe he needed before the lights came back on.

Drago had slipped into the bus, and had taken the small bottle of sulfuric acid he'd created, and carefully concealed it into the seam of the third row seat. It was important that he covered up the small rip as much as possible. The guards always did a thorough check of the bus for any possible weapons, or things the inmates might use to escape.

He'd used a ballpoint pen the guard gave to him, as getting a knife would've taken too much time to acquire. And was harder to conceal. Making a small incision in the weakest part of the fabric, and forcing the bottle into it.

During the checks, it would go unnoticed, as the bottle was small enough to be submerged in the cotton, and would not make a lump.

Now, Drago retrieved the bottle as his heart pounded with adrenaline. Breathing a sigh of relief that it had not been discovered and removed. What he would do next, would be cruel yet necessary. He had no choice.

Drago opened the bottle, and swiftly splashed a few drops on his partners' arms. Knowing the immediate burn of pain would awaken him.

The man woke in a screeching cry, crazed and shaking in his seat, as his arms began to smoke and steam, the skin burning away slowly.

Drago jumped into action without hesitation.

"Help! Oh my god, this man needs help!"

The guard in the first row turned around abruptly, and shot up out of his seat. His eyes wide in panic as he saw the smoke rising from the prisoner. They normally had a protocol for emergencies that happened on the bus, but it was those first few seconds of panic that Drago was relying on. He didn't give the guard a chance to think.

"Hurry! Get over here, he's burning up! It's almost got me too!" Drago pulled at his chains acting with terror, as he pleaded with the guard to help them.

The guard hesitated for only a moment. Seeing the smoke, he called out to the driver anxiously, and signaled him.

"Sean, we got a code red! We need to call it in. Stop at the nearest exit and call in the medics."

The driver looked up in the rearview mirror, saw the smoke, and immediately took a turn for Balys Pond, while speaking into the walkie talkie.

Meanwhile, the first guard approached Drago and the gyrating man cautiously, his face filled with terror, watching the burns appear on the prisoner's arms.

"What the hell is wrong with him?!" The guard shouted at Drago, his hand slightly moving over to his gun.

Drago knew he had to act fast, or lose the element of surprise. He started shaking his chains, and acting crazy, as if his fear was out of control.

"I don't know, man! Just get me away from him, before it gets on me! Look! It's spreading!"

The guard saw the smoke and horrible burns, and took in Drago's panic. He grunted in finality, and rushed forward, taking out his key and unlocking Drago's chains at his hands and feet.

As the guard stood up to move Drago away from the screaming prisoner, he was met with a face of stone and death.

Drago grabbed the keys, and simultaneously splashed some of the acid into the guard's face. Shoving him into the seat with a fierceness, as he cried out in abject pain, just as Drago raced to the front of the bus and opened the iron fence separating the driver.

All of this happened within exactly two minutes.

The driver was just pulling up along the road with the body of water, and looked up into the rearview mirror too late. His hand reached for his gun, but not before the acid flew into his eyes and face. The guard screamed, his hand jerking reflexively on the wheel. The bus careened sideways, and swayed at a dangerous speed. Drago tried to get to the doors, but the momentum of the bus was going too fast. The vehicle turned violently, and lost its balance.

The impact of the water slammed Drago further into the bus, as it broke the surface, and plummeted heavily to the bottom.

Chapter Two

Only a few days later in Jarratt, VA

The news is what brought her here. To this run down dilapidated place, that looked as if it was built from a hole within the wall. The small town bar didn't even have music playing, and the occupants were all characters and drifters that preferred to remain anonymous.

She'd made her best efforts to blend in, concealing her shapely curves, as they were covered in baggy jeans, and an oversized sweatshirt. She was only there to do an assessment of the area. Not a pickup. At least not as yet. She'd already taken more than ten men in the surrounding region, and didn't want to call too much attention to herself. The alarm wasn't going up as of yet, because she was very careful in her work. However, living as long as she did, she'd learned that caution kept you alive.

Cassandra Martin nursed her fourth drink as she waited. Subtly watching the doors out of the corners of her eyes. She'd seen his picture enough times on the news channels to recognize him, even if he wore a clever disguise.

Cassandra turned back to her drink and adjusted her baseball cap. It wasn't what the news had reported that had drawn her there, and picked her interest. To the contrary. It was what they hadn't said that was keeping her glued to that chair. She'd been hanging around for over two hours now. Any much longer, and people would start to ask questions.

Just as she'd begun to consider staking out another location, the front doors opened slowly, and a tall man walked in.

Immediately, without even looking into his face, Cassandra knew that he was the one she'd been waiting for. The man wore all black. Black jeans, black polo shirt, and had a trimmed yet full beard curving a hard and unreadable face. He strolled over to the bar a few chairs down from her, and ordered a drink. Cassandra noticed the deep bass in his voice, and her fingers curled around her glass imperceptibly.

Never once looking over at him, she was able to view him with her hyper senses. It was like opening up an antenna in her mind, and tuning into his channel. The resounding static confused and baffled her. Cassandra was shocked, a feeling that she was very unfamiliar with. For some reason, she could not get a fix on his aura. She couldn't see his soul.

When the news report came in, she'd been in her hotel room in Richmond, Virginia. She'd just finishing bagging and disposing of another dark one, and was feeling unusually bored. The 'dark ones' are what she called the black souled men she captured and took to be judged and assessed. They were all she'd ever encountered. Men with souls so dark, it was like seeing black holes that walked and breathed. But after doing it for the past eighteen years, she was growing bored of the easy prey. There was never any challenge. Never any break from the monotony. She found herself killing more viciously just to get a thrill, and would have to bring herself back from the brink of turning into one of the empties.

Cassandra feared that the darkness was calling her each day, her bitterness of mankind and their callous ways of living, causing her to forget her vows and her purpose. But she could not let that happen. She was a gates keeper. Holder of the sacred key. Her people needed her. But she knew that time was running out. She had only two more years on earth, before she would be forced to go underground again. Because there were rules she had to abide by. A gates keeper could only roam the earth for twenty years, before the humans began to detect her presence. The humans, although far less advanced than her kind, they were cunning and clever. They had succeeded before in wiping out her species. Cassandra would not allow them to do it again.

As she'd drained most of the blood of her latest victim, leaving him weak enough to take into custody, the news report came on and indicated that a bus holding two convicts scheduled to receive death by lethal injection, had crashed into Balys Pond, in Jarratt Virginia.

The clip showed that there were no survivors. It listed that there were two guards on the bus, along with the prisoners. Then they showed the photos of all the deceased men.

When Cassandra had seen the photo of the man known to the media as Jason Freeman, she'd immediately gone on alert. Every sense within her body had tingled and began to burn as if she was on fire. It was usually the signal that there was a dark soul nearby. But she had never experienced the reaction as she did just then. She'd known right away that the man being called Jason Freeman was not dead. He had to be still alive, in order for her to sense him like this. And he must be truly evil indeed, if he had pulled off such a feat, and managed to fake his own death.

Cassandra had become intrigued. She quickly took care of her recent victim, teleported from the hotel and took him through the gates, in which of course he was found guilty. The man's anguished screams of torture filled her with a thrill of satisfaction.

Once she was done, she had made plans to track down this mystery man whom everyone thought was dead. She would find him, assess his soul, and then have him tortured more slowly than the others. The anticipation gave her renewed hope and vigor.

Now, as she sat a few seats away from the man in question, she was confused and a bit dismayed at the outcome. Why couldn't she see into this stranger? Suddenly her mild intrigue had gone into full blown interest, and fascination. She needed to find out more about this one, and just what he had to hide. It was time to try a different method.

***

Drago had entered the bar already knowing what to expect. A few stragglers, some inquisitive looks, but then the total disinterest, as every one of the men and women inside preferred anonymity. It was why he'd chosen it.

After laying low for a few days following the crash, Drago had gone to the secret location he'd privately hired someone on the outside to locate.

With his instructions, the guy had buried a locked box, in which a second man he'd hired held the key to. Neither man had known each other, or what the key or box held value for. They'd never met up or ever saw each other. The man with the key buried it in a different location, then the man with the box. Therefore, neither guy would be compelled to open a box in which held important meaning to him alone.

They'd been paid handsomely. Once Drago felt the coast was clear, and everyone thought he was dead, something he'd made certain of by ensuring the nearby alligators would tear into most of the remains. While he provided a fourth, already dead body, that he had also hired someone to bury in the lake. Drago had made sure all the corpses were thoroughly mauled by the alligators. Too desecrated to be identified. Later, he had emerged from his hideout deep in the woods, and located the spot where the key was buried first. Unbeknownst to the hired men, both buried items were not that far from each other. But each task had been performed three days apart, over two years ago. So no one would ever be the wiser, or draw connection between the locations.

Drago had retrieved the key, exactly where he had instructed it to be. Then dug up the box. Inside the object were new Identification, and other important items he needed.

The rest had been simple. As he'd walked into town as a free man no one seemed to recognize. Amazing what the power of the media could do. Since everyone assumed he was dead, no one would even think to connect his face with a deceased one's. However, Drago was still a cautious man. And so he'd chosen the inconspicuous bar as the perfect way to gain information on what he was looking for. Just because he was out of prison, didn't mean that he stopped pursuing the reason that had put him there in the first place.

As Drago ordered a drink, and sat down wrapped in his musings, he began to feel the most uncomfortable sensation. Immediately, his highly trained senses went on red alert. And Drago fell into stealth mode. Using the mirror that lined the back of the bar to watch and analyze the entire room. Very carefully, he watched every man and woman, dismissing them as harmless or unimportant. Until his distinguished pupils landed onto the overly bundled up figure in the corner. Drago's eyes rested on the individual, not sure at first whether it was a man or woman. Their head was bent low, and the baseball cap covered their face. All he could see was a round smooth cheek. But the clothes were what struck him as odd. It was obvious the person was trying hard not to be seen, and in doing so, stood out like a sore thumb.

Who would choose to wear a sweatshirt, in the summertime, at over ninety degree weather outside? And big bulky jeans that didn't seem to fit?

Drago frowned as he watched the figure trying hard to keep their face hidden. Whoever they were, they needed a crash course in anonymity. Cause they were terrible at it.

Suddenly, without warning, the figure stood up abruptly and turned to leave the bar. Drago was thrown off balance, as the action was so fast, he'd never gotten a chance to see their face. Before he knew what was happening, the person was walking towards the front doors.

Drago was so shocked, he sat up straight just in time to see them walk out of the bar.

"What the hell?" He cursed silently under his breath, as he paid his bill quickly and hurried to go after the individual. No one had ever gotten the drop on him like that. Not when he was actively watching them! Who the heck was this person?

Drago was not about to let them get away. He was about to find out, one way or another.

Chapter Three

Drago bolted out of the bar, and took a few steps outside onto the sidewalk. It was now dusk, and the sky gave off a deep purple and yellow blended tapestry, across the sunset. The street was quiet, there were no cars or pedestrians that roamed this pathway. The bar was chosen by those who preferred to be hidden for a reason. It remained secluded away from the rest of population. Tucked deep in a part of the woods that would never draw attention, or unwanted perusal. There was a road that led to the bar, that eventually connected to the main highway of I95. The parking lot and small entryway sidewalk outside the bar, led to a pathway within the woods, which would take you back to civilization. If you made it that far. The woods in these parts, held a number of secrets and riffraff that decent folk would never dare to enter or encounter. It was why only a few knew about the small hangout simply named: The Place. Drago had gone there looking for some answers. But now, he was searching for a mystery.

He paused cautiously, and surveyed his surroundings. The parking lot was completely vacant, except for two cars parked over to the side. There were no people loitering on the path, and no suspicious looking character that had left the bar in such haste. He was alone. But Drago didn't buy it. How could the stranger have disappeared so quickly?

Everything inside Drago was telling him something was off about this, and to proceed carefully. But just as he was about to head back into the bar, a movement to the far left caught his eye.

There was a woman walking towards him. She wasn't headed for the bar, she was coming directly for him, and Drago knew it as he surely knew his own name. Because as he looked at her, there wasn't much else he could really remember in that brief moment. It was as if time literally stood still, then slowed down, as the most perfect creation that he'd ever witnessed, seemed to glide towards him. As if her feet never touched ground. But that would be impossible.

Her skin was as smooth as porcelain. A mixture between light brown and faded butter cream. Her cheekbones were high, and curved delicately within the most luscious full lips he'd ever seen. Lips that were blood red, and smirking, ever slightly. But her eyes...

Drago's heart began to race, as his mind fought to grasp some sort of control. To make sense of it all. Her body was sinfully made. So many curves and dips that a man was sure to die trying to find them all. She was wrapped in the tightest jeans, thighs and hips so accentuated, that he could see every glorious pressure point. The tank top she had on was a pale blue, matching her jeans, and hugged onto two of the most perfectly sculpted breasts, that any artist would've given his soul to create. And her hair was kept loose around her oval face. Black thick waves of curly seduction, cascading around her shoulders and covering part of that beautiful face. But it was her eyes that held him captive. Eyes that commanded he listen to her. Watch her. Deep green and emerald glowing eyes that whispered for him to obey....

Wait a second. Obey? Drago's befuddled brain groggily woke up at the thought of surrendering something he couldn't quite explain. His formidable will power took control and shattered the undaunting spell the woman seemed to have over him. By the time he shook his head to clear it, she was standing in front of him, a confused look on her face, and her small hands sitting on her shapely hips. She was annoyed and perplexed.

"Who the hell are you?" Both of them said the words simultaneously.

Drago tried not to break out into a grin, at what he suddenly seemed to find very amusing. This was the best interaction he'd had since he could ever remember. But the woman in question was far from amused. She frowned, and her cute nose wrinkled in frustration.

"I ask the questions, sir. Not you. Now who the hell are you, and why are you following me?"

The woman looked him directly in the eyes, and demanded a response. Drago could tell she was used to having her way. It would be interesting to see what she would do when thwarted.

"I think you have your customers lined up wrong, chick." Drago said casually, hooking his thumbs within his pockets. He nodded his head in a dismissive manner, and smirked at her.

"Go run along now, little lady. I've got more important things to do right now, than talk to underage girls out beyond their curfew."

He said the words ever so cavalier. But never noticed the change in the atmosphere as he did so. Several things suddenly seemed to happen all at once.

One moment Drago was standing up, the next he was flat on his back. The beautiful woman he had taken for an inconspicuous call girl, had moved so swiftly, she flipped his legs from under him, and was now coming in for a lethal blow to the head.

Drago's instincts kicked in at supercharge, and deflected a punch that landed into the pavement behind him. He heard the ground rumble, and was secretly amazed at the impact within those little hands.

Reassessing her quickly, Drago caught the woman's arm and flung her body like paper, landing a quick and paralyzing jab to the neck. A blow that normally rendered his victims powerless.

However, the woman simply rolled as she fell to the ground, and bent her body in a way that propelled her to her feet once again. Drago didn't have time to allow the shock to distract him. She came at him lightning fast, her eyes glowing strangely, and the air felt heavy and suffocating.

Instinctively, Drago's highly trained skills were alerting him to the fact that the woman was manipulating the atmosphere somehow. A distraction that would give her the advantage to gain the upper hand.

Closing out the interference, Drago crouched low as she whipped into the air with a swinging kick, and he turned, jutting out his leg and landing a cracking blow to her spine. The woman cried out in shocked pain, as she fell to the floor. She rolled and then jumped to her feet. Her anger was now palpable.

Drago knew in that moment he had to subdue her, and quickly. Because whatever she was doing with her fists, as they balled up and were beginning to glow, would be the end of him.

Going with his gut reaction, Drago withdrew two small knives from his back pocket, and flung them swiftly at the woman's hands. The blades imbedded themselves deep into the palms of her fists, successfully disabling the increasing glow that was coming from them.

The woman screamed in morbid pain, as she was momentarily distracted, and raised her hands to remove the knives. Drago used that brief second to land a flying kick to her jaw, that sent her spiraling across the pavement, to collapse onto the ground. Her body remained still, for the moment out cold.

Breathing heavily, with a slight gash seeping from his head, he held his aching side as he walked over to the still form. Drago eyed the woman cautiously as she lay on the ground, and turned her over with his foot.

She was still unconscious, but from what he'd seen she wouldn't be for long. The knives were still stuck in her hands, and he could see the blood seeping from them. Ultimately, he was certain the woman would be alright, whoever she was. But he had a lot of questions now. Questions he needed her to answer. He couldn't just leave her there in the parking lot. Even though it was obvious she could handle herself well.

Drago had to admit, he was impressed with her. But the woman was deadly. And he believed she had targeted him for a specific reason. There was no way to know, unless he got it out of her.

Drago stared at her perfect voluptuous form. Even knocked out, she was stunning. But none of that mattered now. Now he had to figure out what to do with her. He needed to know exactly why she had targeted him, and then tried to kill him.

Chapter Four

Cassandra opened her eyes slowly, and immediately felt the ache in her hands. The knives had been removed, and there were bandages around both her wrists. She knew the wounds were already healing, now that she was awake. The skin was slowly closing itself back up. However, she had lost a good amount of blood. And she needed a replacement fast, or she would be weak, and at the mercy of her captor.

Thinking of her captor Cassandra turned her head to assess her surroundings. She was bound and tied by rope, around her arms and legs. Secured to a chair in a rundown motel room. She was situated next to the single bed, which had a small end table next to it, and an odd looking black box placed upon it. There was a small dresser in the room and a lopsided TV that stood on it. A door that was slightly ajar, led to a small bathroom on the side. But Cassandra's eyes were more focused on the bed. And what was lying within it.

The man who had so brilliantly overpowered her, was laying down in the bed with his hands behind his head. He had removed his black polo shirt and shoes, and only kept his pants on. And oh praise the gods, what a sight he made.

Cassandra stared at what had to be the most perfect piece of human male she had ever seen. He was not overly large. No. But he was cut and toned so right. Every ripple of muscle begged to be touched and traced. His chest was padded with hardened sinew, and carved into a perfectly placed set of six pack, abdominal heaven. A delicious path of black hair lined the bottom of his stomach and disappeared into those sexy jeans. Covering legs that were strong and brawny.

Cassandra didn't know that her eyes had begun to change color slightly, turning from emerald green, to a lovely shade of deep caramel chocolate. Her breath came in short spurts, and her hands became sweaty and twitchy. As if she yearned to touch...to taste. Never before had she felt this way. In all her two hundred years of living, and her eighteen years on earth, she had never felt so.... alive. Exhilarated, Cassandra turned back to look at his face, and saw that he was awake. Watching her watch him. The slight satisfied male smirk on his lips, told her he knew exactly what she was thinking.

Humiliated for the first time in her existence, Cassandra's eyes turned back to their normal green, and glowed with a heated anger. She balled her fists, but then remembered she was too weak to free herself. The blasted human garbage!

Drago watched the beautiful vixen as she sat tied to the chair, assessing how she seemed to calmly evaluate her situation, and search for the best way to outmaneuver him. It was fascinating to see, to say the least. He had never met a woman who was as methodical and calculating as this one. But then again, Drago had already surmised that she was far more than just a woman. But exactly what she was, he intended to find out.

Getting up from the bed, Drago ignored her and turned over to his black box. He retrieved a strange looking small pendant, shaped in the form of a silver ball, almost like a pearl, but with strange colors within it. Quietly, he placed the pendant onto a thin chain and draped it around his neck. Then putting his shirt on, he bent over to put on his sneakers, all the while systematically waiting to see what she would do. Drago felt that ignoring a woman was the greatest weapon man created, when controlling a female. Most women seemed to think they held the crown on the silent treatment. But for Drago, the complete lack of attention to an obviously beautiful woman, was the best way to break through to her insecurities, and get her to do anything you wanted. It took skills, it took ingenuity, it took....

Drago turned to see that Cassandra had already bitten through half of her ropes, and was almost free.

"Shit!" He cursed and leaped over the bed, just as Cassandra ripped one of the bottom legs of the chair off and swung it at him, using the deadly point to try and pierce his skin.

The chair had collapsed sideways, and she landed on her face, but her left arm was free. She was in the process of removing the rest of her binds when Drago fell onto her, and yanked the chair leg from her hand. But not before he received a blinding blow to the head, and a powerful jab to the ribs.

Drago could only imagine what would have happened if she was at her full strength! He had underestimated her. A mistake he would never make again.

"Enough! Stop fighting me! You'll only hurt yourself more." Drago used his weight to pin her down, and held her free arm behind her back in a painful grip. He knew he was hurting her, but the woman would simply not relent. Her face was a mask of fury and rage, but her eyes were filled with pain and...fear?

Drago held still waiting for the fight to drain out of her. She was weak and had lost some blood, but yet and still, she fought as if she was a caged and wild animal. But it was her fear that gave him pause. She hadn't seemed to be threatened by him in the least. So what was she afraid of?

Cassandra finally stopped her struggling, and panted in frustration. Her arm was bent backwards by this solid brute of muscle, and the chair and ropes made it difficult to move. If only he was close enough to bite. But he wisely kept his face just above her own. She wasn't used to this. Who was this human? How was it he was able to overpower her? What did he want with her? For the first time Cassandra felt the beginning prickles of fear, as she lay helpless underneath him, just as any normal human woman. More than likely he would rape and kill her. And her people would never know what had become of her. They would all just wither away and die.

Helpless in her new unbidden emotions, the glimmering shine of tears swam in her eyes for a brief moment, something she wasn't even aware of, before Cassandra closed them and turned her face away in shame.

Drago felt a wrenching pain to his heart. If there was anything that he couldn't take, it was seeing a woman's genuine tears. And he knew these were true. The fact that she tried to hide them only solidified the fact.

He made a quick decision, and decided to change his method.

"I'm going to let you out of these ropes, so I can see to your wounds, and we can talk. But if you try to fight me, or if you try to escape, I'll bleed you out slowly. I will cut you so that your death will be a painful and tortuous one. All I want to do is talk. Do I make myself clear?"

Drago waited for a response from her. She kept her eyes closed, but the deeply indrawn sigh and the slight jerk of her head was enough for him.

Cautiously, still not trusting her, Drago released her from her bonds and helped her out of the chair to sit on the bed. It was evident she was definitely weaker. But her face should not be that pale, and her lips were now a darkened blue. The wounds on her hands had reopened, and were now bleeding profusely, as she collapsed onto the bed. She began to cough and hack, and her body was shaking as if she was cold.

Drago began to panic, realizing she must be going into some sort of shock. He had no medical kit with him, and he couldn't risk leaving her to get help.

"Fuck! What the hell am I supposed to do? I didn't sign up for this shit!" Drago shouted out loud to himself as she trembled violently on the bed. Her eyes beginning to roll to the top of her head. He could just walk away right now and leave her there. She wasn't his problem. She was probably going to die anyway. What did he care? But the problem was Drago did in fact care. It was because of him she was like this. He couldn't just leave her there to die. No matter how much he wanted to, there was something holding him back.

Drago grabbed some towels from the bathroom and raced back over to her. The bed was almost soaked in her blood. She was losing too much! He sat down and cradled her body into his lap, trying to wrap the towels over the now seeping wounds on her hands. The previous bandages, he'd made from ripping part of the sheets, were now soaked and useless. He could do nothing but watch her bleed out, her skin turning greyish, as he held her body in his arms. She was going to die. And there was nothing he could do to save her.

Drago felt an unreasonable burst of imponent rage. He could not let her go. He'd only just found her.

"Tell me, what should I do? Tell me how to help you!" Drago was speaking to himself out loud, but it was the gargled response he received that shocked him out of his dilemma.

"I need…. blood…."

Drago looked down at the woman's beautiful yet deathly pale face, and saw that her eyes were staring up at him. They were only open to mere slits, and he could see she was fighting for control, but her bleeding hand was now gripping his shirt in a death grip, and there was desperation in her half open eyes. A look that Drago knew instinctively she'd never had before.

"Blood? You mean like a transfusion? I would have to take you to the hospital for that. They ask a lot of questions, but maybe I can get someone to---"

"No! Not a hospital, you fool! I need blood now. Your blood. I need to...drink it.... now...."

Drago became silent as he stared at her, her words made no sense at all. It was obvious she was delusional.

"Listen, don't try to talk, I'll find a way to get you some help, I know a few people and...."

Drago's voice faded off as he watched two amazingly lethal incisors extend from within the woman's open mouth. Her teeth grew like daggers, and her eyes turned a glowing red. A hungry and starving look appeared on her pale face, as her head now moved back and forth in agitation and discomfort. He watched as her nails grew in length, slightly ripping a hole in his shirt.

Drago leaped from the bed, and threw her from him to crash against the pillows. She began to moan and clutch her stomach, gripping the sheets. She looked up at him, as her body trembled helplessly. The pleading look was in her eyes as the strength left her body. The whisper was her final plea.

"Help me...."

Drago watched as her head lolled to the side, and her body went limp. She was no longer moving.

"Fuck!!" Drago shouted into the air, as he raced over to the bed to do what should not have been possible.

He took one of his knives and opened a gash on his arm. Gently leaning her head onto his lap, Drago slowly led her blue lips to his flesh, and waited to see what would happen next.

Chapter Five

Cassandra felt the sweet taste of blood touch her lips, and a jolt of power and ravenous need filled her body. Latching onto his arm with a feverish greed, her tongue swirled a seductive path onto his skin, before her teeth sank deep into the warm muscular flesh.

Drago grunted for only a brief moment from the shock of pain, before the most erotic sensation erupted within him. The feel of her moist lips sucking and tasting his blood, drawing from him what she needed, was the most intense and purely sexual experience he'd ever received. He closed his eyes as his hands buried themselves in her luscious curls. Trailing her cheekbones, and following a path to her beautiful round breasts. He cupped the weight of it through the fabric of her tank top. She wore no bra, so her nipple was hard and rising to his attention. Drago squeezed the delectable flesh, as his body began to feel elevated. He was so deep within the chains of her lustful touch, that he was completely unaware she was draining his life away.

But Cassandra was fully aware. His blood was so sweet. Sweeter than any she'd ever tasted before. It was addictive. She wanted it all. To take his essence and make it her own. To take his life....

But then his hand touched her face. It was such a gentle touch, so tender and sincere. A caress of trust. Of desire. His fingers explored the depths of her breasts, and Cassandra felt the blood in her veins shudder. Her body reacted to his touch, as if he had a power that claimed her under its own spell.

Cassandra wrenched her lips away in a panic, before she could take his life. She moved away from him quickly, not wanting to be near him, or feel him again. What manner of human man was this? She could no longer just kill him, even if she wanted to. She had to bring him through the gate for judgement. But the problem was, she could not see his soul. She could not just label him, as she normally did with the others, and discard him to be destroyed. She knew that would be his ultimate fate. But in order to take him, she needed to see him and judge him. And so far, she couldn't even stand the feel of him.

Cassandra, now at full strength, moved over to the other side of the room, to sit in the second chair available. There was a small table she hadn't noticed before, tucked away into the far corner of the room. She sat at that table now, and waited patiently for him to come to his senses. He was stronger than most human males, and it didn't take him long to regain his composure.

Now calm and in control once again, Cassandra watched the man that saved her life with hooded and guarded eyes. As he sat up on the bed, and held his head to clear it, she posed the question that was foremost in her mind, and got straight to the point.

"Who the hell are you? And what were you doing at The place?" Her words came out clipped and cool. There was no sign of the vulnerability he had glimpsed only moments ago.

Drago took a deep breath and looked up at her. So they were back at square one again, as if all that crap, and the recent trip his soul had just taken to mars, never occurred. Well, two could play at this game. And it was one he was very good at.

Drago cleared his throat, and leaned back nonchalantly on the bloody bed, only vaguely realizing she had somehow closed the wound on his arm, as if the erotic touch from heaven had never existed. But that was irrelevant now.

"I don't think you're in any position to ask me the questions. I believe you're the one that needs to do some talking. You tried to kill me, remember?" Drago replied sarcastically, watching the irritation appear on her lovely face, which was now back to its soft butter cream glow.

"Why don't I just break the ice, so we don't have to go through this song and dance again, ok? I'll go first. My name is really Drago Brown, and I'm---"

"An escaped convict who faked his own death. Killed the other passengers on the bus, and covered his tracks like the expert con artist he is. I know what you are, Drago. Now, are you going to tell me who you really are?"

Cassandra had smoothly interrupted him, and laid out all the cards on the table. Not only was Drago thoroughly impressed, he was now reclassifying her as a worthy opponent.

"And how would you know all that about me, mystery lady? Unless you are the one who was stalking me?"

Before Cassandra could reply, Drago carefully lifted both knives from within his box. He placed them onto his lap, but kept his hands within inches of the daggers. Letting Cassandra know that if she tried anything, his already proven speed would be utilized again, and she would find herself wounded, or in that helpless position she didn't want to be in.

Cassandra was not willing to test that theory once again. She nodded her head in respect, and gave a small smirk at the apparent sharpness of the man's wit.

"My name is Cassandra Martin. I heard of you through the public media while traveling in Jarratt on...business."

Drago noticed the slight hesitation when she said 'business' and he carefully tucked that knowledge away to dissect later.

"I'm searching for someone. And you had fit the description of who I'm looking for. I need you to come with me, so I can find out if you...can match the position my organization is looking to fill."

Drago sat nonchalantly, his gaze never leaving hers, and watching her every move. Listening to her very weak explanation, it was easy to surmise that the woman was lying through her sharp teeth. But if he was going to find out the truth, he would need to play along. Because obviously, this woman wasn't normal. She drank blood, and her eyes glowed for Pete's sake. The real question was, what did she want with him? It wasn't to kill him, because she had ample opportunity to do that. Drago sat up and dropped all pretense of chivalry. It was time to get down to business.

"Let's get one thing straight, Cassandra. If that's your real name." Drago said flippantly. "I'm not going anywhere with you. And secondly, that story you just told me was bullshit. Straight up. So I don't know what sort of sick game or cult you may be into, where maybe you guys drain the blood of cows or something, or even into some sick satanic worship. Count me out. All I want to know is, how do you know so much about me? And if I hear another lie, I'm walking out that door and you won't be able to find a trace of me."

He was serious. She could see it in his very alluring topaz and hazel green eyes. Cassandra frowned as she found the color very similar to her own. And just as mesmerizing. Focusing her thoughts, she calculated the best way in her mind to subdue this man to her will. Her mind control was not working on him. And he was quick enough with those weapons that she could easily be matched, if she went up against him in a fight. She had never had this problem before and had not been trained for this. The order never taught her what to do if she could not see and overpower the soul. That never happened before in all their entire existence. Cassandra could think of nothing else to do. She was going to try and seduce him in the normal human way. And she would tell him what he wanted to hear.

"Alright, here's the truth, handsome. Yes, I was following you. I watched you in the bar and wanted some company. It was my normal night to work, so I had stepped outside to change clothes. To become more attractive for you...."

Cassandra stood up slowly, and began to remove her shirt. Her perfectly rounded creamy breasts, were bare for his perusal and display.

Drago's mouth lost all saliva, and his throat hitched, as he stared at the most beautiful set of breasts he'd ever seen. She was a siren, dangerous and tempting at the same time. Walking towards him slowly, as her body seemed to call him, reaching inside and digging deep within the depths of his soul.

Drago's heart accelerated, as Cassandra now stood in front of him. A sensual offering of desire.

His face remained impassive as he stared at her beauty. His hands aching to touch the soft texture of the moistened skin.

Drago could feel his resistance begin to crumble; the moment Cassandra touched his face. His heart thudded within his chest, and some inner self preservation rose up within his mind at the last possible moment. He moved her hand from his face with great effort, and got up from the bed, putting as much distance between them as necessary.

"Nice try. But I'm not in the need for female company right now. So if that's all you're looking for, then I'm sorry. I've got more important things I need to take care of." Drago said this as he was turned away, so she couldn't see how he was struggling to regain his composure.

Cassandra was through playing games. Pissed, she put her shirt back on, and placed her hands on her hips. Playtime was over.

"Listen, human male garbage. I'm done with this primitive way of communicating. I have a job to do.

And I'm going to do it. I need to take you with me. Now, you can choose to come with me willingly, or by force. Your choice. Either way, we are going to the Carpathian Mountains together."

Drago was about to give one of his snide remarks, when the words shriveled up and died in his mouth. Did she just utter what he thought she said? Could it be possible she was the missing link to what had landed him in jail in the first place?

He had to calm his wayward thoughts and make sure of what she was telling him. Perhaps there was some mistake. He turned around to face her abruptly.

"Did you say, the Carpathian Mountains? Where exactly are you referring to? What are you talking about?" Drago chose his words to her carefully. He needed to be certain.

Cassandra rolled her eyes impatiently, too annoyed to notice his stiff body posture, or his now suspicious eyes.

"I didn't stutter, you fool. Yes, the Carpathian Mountains! My home. The only one the matters, near the Morskie, Oko. In Poland. That's where I'm taking you. And we've already wasted too much time. I've never been away this long on a hunt. My people are probably worried sick and...."

Cassandra's words trailed off as she realized all that she'd just said. She stood shocked and frozen with confusion. Why had she given all that information to this human? She never lost control. Never!

But Drago was staring at her with a calm look on his face. He seemed different now, more at ease. The look in his eyes were...hard to place. But his next words baffled her even more.

"You're right. We've already wasted a lot of time. I'll go with you. But we're going to need some supplies. That's a very long travel from here."

Cassandra frowned as Drago headed into the bathroom and turned on the water, as if the conversation was over. But then again, she'd gotten what she'd wanted hadn't she? He was coming with her. No arguments, or further fight was needed. She should be relieved.

But as Cassandra watched the calm human male called Drago methodically get ready for their trip, her internal instincts were warning her that there was danger near. But she could not fathom where it could possibly be coming from.

Chapter Six

The Tatra Mountains, Morskie Oko, Poland

It was strictly forbidden to venture outside of the protective walls, unless you were of the ordained calling. There were none that even knew what the existence of the above world looked like. They were taught and fed only by the sacred gate keepers. The highly gifted ones who were chosen to go above ground and bring back sustenance for all of them. They were not allowed to feed on human blood. It was said that to taste it, would drive them all with a burning need to hunt. And break their ancient vow of seclusion. Only the gifted ones were strong enough to venture out, and feast on the humans without fear of being tuned into the dark empties. Those that the humans were apt to name, the vampires. It was a law that had been obeyed without question. Handed down from the queen herself. And until that moment, there was never a reason to even consider breaking it. Until now.

Catalina moved with a deftness and made certain not to disturb the pressure points built to set off the alarms within the rocky grounds.

The south tunnel was only accessible for the gifted ones. The most powerful females of their species who were trained from young, on how to leave and enter through the mouth of the buried caves. Not only was it designed to keep intruders out, and kill anyone who dared to breach their sanctuary. It was also created to keep them within. A dark fortress that felt more and more like a prison to some.

Catalina paused, as she used her ruby colored eyes to see within the darkness. All Carpathian women could see within the color of night. However, the deep blackness of this part of the cave was deliberately orchestrated to confuse human and Carpathians alike. To discourage any from venturing out, the queen had created a thick blanket that only the chosen could see through. Without the special sight, you were completely blind and susceptible to the dangers within the cave walls.

Even though Catalina was not one of the gifted, her spirit sister, Cassandra, had more than equipped her with the secrets she needed to pass through the gate.

Catalina took a deep breath, and used the spell within her mind that Cassandra had given her, to see what was in front of her.

The pathway became clear. Lit with small crystals on the ground, forming a glowing road that narrowed further down to the right. The shiny lit path was very thin. However, outside of the trail of glowing white diamonds, there were steaming red hot coals of earth. Invisible to the naked eyes, they were deadly and would cause instant death, in which the victim would sink into what looked like a quicksand of boiling lava.

Catalina's body began to tremble, as she considered going back. But then she remembered her spirit sister's words. Words she always recited to her before she left for a hunt.

***

"I have no one left, Catalina. You are my only family now. I need you to remember what to do if anything should ever happen to me. It's important you follow my instructions exactly, or you will die. Do you understand?" Cassandra looked into the eyes of the one she'd taken on as her spirit sister.

A custom the Carpathian women had adopted when their race had begun to die off. There were so very few of them left. And the chosen ones all came from a line of females handed down to them at birth. But the last Carpathian male had died hundreds of years ago. And left only a few seeds to be generated. Cassandra was the very last of those seeds. The women could no longer produce at all, and so the hunt for the male humans had increased in vigor.

But the life of the Carpathian female had shortened expeditiously. Going from five hundred or more years, down to a mere two centuries. Cassandra had lost her mother and both her sisters. And now she was the only living Carpathian female that could save them all. But given the amount of time that had already passed, and the very grim outlook of things, Cassandra had chosen to adopt a spirit sister. One whom she would trust as she had done of her own blood. This was supposed to ease the loneliness of seeing the passing of family members. But Cassandra had used the connection with Catalina for other means. An alternative plan that she had sworn her to secrecy.

Catalina nodded her head. Her long sleek black hair falling down to her waist, and her coffee colored skin seemed to glow with excitement, yet fear. Her ruby eyes sparkled as she thought of the secrets Cassandra would tell her. Catalina was still a youngling. A mere seventy years old. But she looked as if she wasn't a day over sixteen. The Carpathian women were known for their youthful looks and everlasting immortal beauty. Cassandra had chosen her for her loyalty and patience. And because of the beautiful spirit she could sense within her. But she hated to place this burden on her shoulders. They had grown so close in between hunts. But the reality needed to be faced. They may never find the help they needed.

Cassandra had whispered to her the secrets of the gifted ones. And had given her specific instructions to perform, if she was gone for longer than a moon cycle. She had taught her well on how to breach the walls of the gate. And what to expect. And how to tell the right time to emerge into the above ground. If she were to come out at the wrong hour, the sun would kill her on contact.

More than terrified, Catalina still accepted the responsibility. She loved Cassandra. And her spirit sister had always returned with no mishaps. Until now.

***

Catalina looked at the ground and trembled. Her tall, slim and elegant form was only dressed in the pale white slip that the women wore, as was the custom. She carried nothing with her but her wits, and the special symbol embedded in her palm, knowing that it was the only thing that would aide her right now.

Steadying her breathing, she kept her eyes on the glowing path, and began to tread softly with her bare feet. Following the trail as it turned towards the right.

As she walked, carefully avoiding the steaming red coals, Catalina could hear the moans before she witnessed the source of its origin. Knowing what to expect, was still not enough to prepare her for the enormity of what she now faced.

Catalina stood frozen as she rounded the corner of the narrow tunnel. Her ruby eyes wide and filled with pain.

The path gave way to a large open space. Big enough to hold a group of the women. But it was not Carpathian women the area was reserved for. This was where the human males were brought to be judged and tried. A place of torture and death.

Catalina watched in stricken shock, as a human male stood naked within a ring of flames. It was the last one Cassandra had recently brought in. He was now in the final stage of judgement. The sentencing. There were three tests in all. And they were usually given swiftly. If the human failed all of them, the finality would be slow and drawn out.

Catalina kept to the shadows as she watched in horror, her hand going over her mouth to cover her helpless whimper.

She watched as one of the Carpathian women stood naked outside of the ring of fire. Staring at the human with eyes of hate. The final test of seduction had been administered, and the human had obviously failed it. The male saw her standing there, and raged at her to free him, now that he realized he was trapped. Calling her all sorts of names and things that Catalina couldn't fathom. But the Carpathian just stood there, and suddenly reached out her hand to touch the flames. As soon as her fingers touched the fire, the flames increased to a raging inferno around the man.

Covering his body, yet not killing him. Just allowing him to feel the pain.

"You have failed the final test, human. Now, you will die slowly." The female stood and watched as the man screamed in pain as his flesh darkened, and peeled. Several dark balls of smoke leaped into the man from four corners, and began to drain him of his blood. Pouring his red life liquid into a strange looking long canister the female now held in her hands.

Catalina watched in frozen disbelief as the Carpathian woman filled the bottle up with the man's blood. But not enough to kill him. She smiled, as the ground opened up beneath him, and plunged him into a deeper pit below.

"You will die, but your blood will give my people life." The female smiled wickedly as she listened to the man's fading howls of terror, as he disappeared into the ground. And then the floor was sealed, and the flames evaporated. As if they were never there.

Shrinking further into the shadows so she wouldn't be seen, Catalina stared as the woman took the bottle of blood and elevated it into the air using her mind, then made it vanish. No doubt concealing it somewhere only she could find it. Then, the woman's white dress reappeared on her body once again, and she performed the ancient Carpathian ritual of repentance, before she herself disappeared from sight.

In the ensuing quiet, the large open area was nothing more than an empty space. The place Catalina now knew was the center of the gate.

Her body was now trembling violently at all she had witnessed and been privy to.

It could not be possible. But Carpathian eyes never lied. It was strictly forbidden to drink the blood of humans. The queen had given those laws to protect them from the greed and hunger of the outside world. Only the gate keepers drank and fed. And it was the hunters who returned with blood of the animals that would feed the rest of their people. It was their way. Their sacred law.

But as Catalina took in all she had seen; she knew that those laws were being broken. And just how long had that female, or any of the others who were selected to judge the human males, fallen victim to the lure of their blood? It was not a good sign for their people. And now, the enormity of Cassandra's words held more weight.

Catalina forced herself to deal with the matter at hand. She focused her attention on the narrow opening that she could feel strange air coming from. A pathway that led up into the top of the tunnel. The entrance of the gate.

Catalina braced herself to make the upward journey, and prepared to do what was necessary in order to save her people.

Chapter Seven

Drago glanced over at Cassandra as she sat in the passenger seat of the stolen vehicle. She was pissed at him, as usual, for yet again gaining the upper hand and maneuvering the first shift to drive. It was after midnight, and she had insisted that she should take the night shift, while he take over the day. But Drago would not budge on that. Since he was the one who'd acquired the vehicle, which was not easy in the small backwards town in Waverly, he would be the one to drive it first. Drago also admitted to himself that he had his own personal reasons for needing to be behind the wheel. And one of them was the unrelenting urge to see her unguarded. Was she really who she alluded to be? It wasn't possible. But he was certainly going to find out.

Cassandra folded her arms in agitation as she sat in the seat. It was extremely discomforting to have someone else do something for her. She wasn't used to it, and didn't like it at all. But she had to admit, secretly she was impressed. She didn't have to use her powers once, since they'd headed out of the motel shortly after nightfall. Drago had shown her the human way of manipulating and gaining control of people, without having to kill them. It was interesting, to say the least. And a bit of a turn on, if she carefully evaluated that line of thought too much. But as she watched him work, he'd managed to get a clean pair of clothes for them from one of the currently empty motel rooms, in which he'd seen a couple that closely resembled their size. She didn't have the heart to tell him she could generate her own clothes. He'd broken into a car rental office without setting off the alarms, and effortlessly hacked into the computers, and placed two fictitious names within the system. He had created a whole agreement for them, without having to kill anyone.

"There are ways to do things without having to cause unnecessary problems." Drago had explained to her when she inquired. She was baffled that they should go through so much trouble. Why not just take the damn car?

"We'd get much farther, if there weren't a bunch of people and cops looking for us." Drago had drawled casually, as if speaking to an idiot.

Cassandra was still fuming over that. Nothing was going as it should be, and what was worse, she could sense the Carpathian call of her spirit sister. Which means that if she didn't get back to the mountains with Drago in time, all hell would break loose.

Drago saw that they were low on gas, and took the next exit. There wasn't an overflow of traffic on the highway at that late hour, but the ones that were, was driving down the interstate at breakneck speed. So it struck Drago's notice, when the black car behind him suddenly turned into the same exit he did. Still following his course, his alarms weren't raised at seeing this, as it was possible the car just happened to be going the same route as he was.

Drago turned down the pathway and headed for the nearest gas station. Noting the black car followed suit.

Saying nothing, he pulled up to one of the pumps and parked the car.

Cassandra huffed out an impatient breath, and looked around. The gas station was very dimly lit and creepy, with only two pumps available. There were no other cars around except for theirs, and a black car that was pulling up to the other pump ahead of them. The station looked as if no one was attending it. It appeared run down, and neglected. There was a faded light on inside, but no evidence anyone was there. For the first time since they left the motel, Cassandra began to feel a smooth prickle of heat along her arms and neck. An ancient Carpathian warning of danger.

She turned her head to alert him.

"Drago...."

He signaled her to be quiet, with a finger to his lips. His eyes never leaving the silent car in front of them. It was a black Nissan Altima. But the windows were all tinted so you could see nothing inside. It remained parked and unmoving, just sitting there in front of the pump. As if waiting.

Drago remained watchful, cautioning Cassandra to do the same. All the while, his hand silently moved to the small black box he always kept with him.

Suddenly, the driver side of the Altima opened up and a man in a navy blue suit stepped out. The passenger side did the same, and a second man wearing a grey suit left the vehicle. Drago watched as both men turned around and stood facing their car. They remained at their vehicle, but their gazes were locked on him.

They had silver chains and small pendants attached to their necks, like Drago wore, but theirs was a symbol of a golden eye. Cassandra noticed this with rising apprehension. And they stood as if waiting for something. With an air of expectancy.

Cassandra turned her suspicious gaze towards Drago. Her senses were rising out of the roof. Something was seriously off here. And it all centered around him.

"Drago...who are those men? Why are they looking at you like they know you? What do they want?"

"You."

As Drago uttered that shocking reply in a chillingly calm voice, the car screeched backwards madly as he stepped on the gas, putting the car in reverse. Cassandra watched as the two men leaped back into their vehicle, and turned their car around to give chase.

"Drago what the hell is going on?! You better give me some answers right now!" Cassandra was thrown against the side, as the car rounded the corner, and headed back onto the highway. Speeding with a screech of tires. The Altima was right behind them.

"Put your seat belt on before you get killed!" Drago shouted at her, as he raced around several vehicles. He held onto the wheel, and stepped on the gas, knowing the car behind them would never stop. He would have to lose them and fast. He looked into the rearview mirror, and saw they were gaining on them. But even worse, there were two other black cars that had joined in the race, and were busily speeding down the highway. Now there were three on his tail. He needed to get off this lane and find a busy street he could disappear in, but he was in unfamiliar territory. His options were low.

Drago narrowly missed an eighteen wheeler truck, as he careened the car into oncoming traffic. Vehicles screeched and two cars flipped over each other trying to avoid collision. Drago jerked the car onto the side and crossed over the junction, getting side swiped at the tail by an oncoming minivan.

"Drago!"

Cassandra cried out as their vehicle went spinning, two cars blaring their horns as they came within inches of hitting them.

Drago kept the wheel, and forced the car onto the road again, crashing into the highway traffic, and regaining control of the vehicle.

"Stay down and shut the fuck up!" Drago snapped at her, as two of the vehicles were now behind them once again. They were like terminators. It would be near impossible to shake them, but he had to try.

Suddenly, one of the passengers in the second car stuck their hand out, and threw something at their vehicle. Drago slammed forward into the wheel, as one of the tires blew out. The car began to skid sideways, and it was hard to maintain control of it.

Drago's heart raced as he knew what they'd done. Next, they would take out all tires until they had crashed and were killed, unless he surrendered now. Unless he gave them what they wanted. Breathing hard, he desperately tried to think of a way out, as the car crisscrossed on the road.

Cassandra looked over at him, and saw the desperation on his face. They were trapped. And though she didn't know who those men were, Drago had indicated they wanted her. Well, that was never going to happen. He would have a lot of explaining to do later, but for now, she needed to get them out of there. But how, when she couldn't seem to teleport with him?

She knew what she had to do. It was risky, and would cause a lot of attention, which she tried to avoid, but there was no other choice.

Cassandra sat back in the seat, and closed her eyes. When they opened again, they were silver orbs of glowing light. Her fists were balled, and her body began to glow.

Drago only glanced over at her briefly, before the complete shock caused him to drop his hands off the wheel.

"Holy shit. What the hell....?"

He was too stricken to realize he was no longer guiding the car, but Cassandra was now in full control. Drago watched as the car righted itself, and the tire inflated once again. As if it was alive. The two cars behind them suddenly became engulfed in flames. Zigzagging into each other, until they collided with several other vehicles and exploded on impact.

The first car somehow escaped, and was trying to back away from the inferno and retreat. But a large ball of flames manifested within the sky and began to follow the car, as it sped along an exit. The men screamed in fear, as the ball slammed into their vehicle, and sent them exploding into millions of pieces. The road lit up with the light of the flames, and the ensuing pandemonium of all the cars that had been caught within the melee.

Drago watched, stiff and silent, as Cassandra's eyes slowly returned to the usual emerald green, and her body lost the eerie white glow. She blinked a few times, and then turned to him calmly, watching him for a few seconds. The look within her eyes were unreadable to him.

"The nuisance has been taken care of. You can now resume in your driving. We will be having a discussion later on."

Cassandra said the words with an air of dismissal, and then turned back in her seat. Silently watching the road.

Drago, his heart pounding wildly, was wise enough to remain silent for the moment, and take a hold of the wheel that was apparently driving itself anyway.

He focused his mind on the only sane thing he could conjure up.

He had to get them to the first stop point on their map. Because after that display and what she'd just proven, Drago knew now there would be dozens more on their trail.

Chapter Eight

Bristol, Tennessee

They had driven through the night, and dawn was fast approaching. Drago was exhausted after the whiplash and adrenaline of the speed car chase, all down interstate ninety five. But it was Cassandra who was foremost on his mind. Now that he knew she was definitely who he thought she was, he had to get her to a motel immediately. She was looking drained, and starting to get that pale look again. She hadn't said a word since their episode of highway adventures. She'd remained stoically silent, to the point where he constantly kept looking over at her to see if she was still coherent. She didn't press the urgency to him, but somehow Drago believed she knew he understood the importance of getting her inside before the sun rose. And they were running out of time.

Drago saw how she seemed to be growing weaker, and stepped on the gas. He didn't know why it mattered so much to him, but seeing her as anything less than her powerful beautiful self, gripped his chest and squeezed his insides. He didn't bother to examine why.

Turning into the exit he'd memorized with the map in his mind, Drago took the road to the hotel that was the located in the most remote spot he could find. They were in Bristol, Tennessee now, and the city was far from the backwards town in Waverly. But that was exactly as Drago had planned it. The more noise, the less people tended to notice strangers.

Pulling up to the hotel, he decided quickly to leave Cassandra in the car while he checked in, under the fake names he registered with. No one needed to see her pale and ghostly looking face and strange glassy green eyes. And she was probably too weak to do her camouflaging stunts. So it was up to him.

"Don't move, ok? I need to check us into the room, but I can't have anyone seeing you like this. It would draw too much attention." Drago unhooked his seat belt and turned to her as he said the words in a rush. Growing more alarmed at her appearance.

He touched her face gently, as she leaned her head back on the seat, and moved a strand of hair from her cheek.

His hand grazed the soft smooth skin, and her eyes turned towards his. An unspoken message of trust that neither of them was ready to explain or mention.

Filled with an irrational emotion he couldn't identify, Drago rushed out of the car and hurried into the front office. The sun was starting to peek over the horizon.

Once he quickly took care of the check in, Drago ran back outside to see that the sun was beginning to rise. Panicked, he looked over to the car. Cassandra had her hands on the window, and her face was in pain.

Jumping into action, Drago charged over to the car like a linebacker, stripping off his shirt as he ran. He jerked open her side of the door, and she fell into his arms, her body shaking and in agony.

Taking the shirt, Drago covered her body as much as he could, and lifted her out of the car just as the sun touched the windowpane. Had he been a second later, she would have fried on the spot.

Running towards the back where their room was located, he was thankful he'd had the presence of mind to ask the lady for a room that did not face the horizon.

Drago paused in front of their door, to unlock it. Still holding Cassandra in his arms. He could feel the soft tremors of her body, as she clung to him. Her vulnerability was doing strange things to his emotions.

Entering the room, Drago gently laid her onto the bed and quickly closed the door and all the curtains. Once the room was sufficiently dimmed, he pulled the shirt off of her.

Cassandra looked up at him as he removed his covering. She was so weak; she could hardly move her head. But she was conscious enough to realize what he'd just done for her. He had saved her life. Again. This man she hardly knew. This...human man. She watched him as he adjusted her within the bed, and pulled the covers up to her chin.

"Get your rest." He said gruffly, obviously trying to hide the tender gesture. He then turned away from her and headed back towards the door. I'll bring in the rest of my things, then I have some work to do. We still have a long travel to Texas, where my guy will be waiting to fly us out of the country. So rest up, you'll need your strength."

Drago then left the room without another word, shutting the door firmly behind him.

Cassandra stared at it for a few moments, before the ancient sleep of her people began to call to her. Yes, they had much to discuss. And he was right. She needed to be at full strength for what was ahead of them.

She closed her eyes and sank into the healing sleep of the Carpathians.

***

Cassandra rose to awareness before her eyes even opened. It was her way of assessing the environment around her, and analyzing if there was any danger. It had kept her alive for two centuries and served her well. But the only thing she could sense now was him. The human male that had saved her life. Twice.

She could feel him even before she saw him. He was very silent, and no normal person would even know he was there. But Cassandra could pick up on his heat as if he was radiating it to her directly. It was thick and felt like a warm and soothing blanket. His presence was like a balm to something that had remained stagnant for as long as she could remember.

Opening her eyes, Cassandra leaned up in the bed and pulled the covers off of her. Searching the room for him.

He was sitting in the corner at a desk, only the desk lamp was on, to give him some light as he worked. A small laptop computer was open in front of him, and that strange looking black box was on the desk as well, partially open among a notebook pad he was writing in.

Cassandra stared at him for a few pleasurable moments, enjoying the way his tightly toned body was hunched over the computer in concentration. He had left the cotton shirt off, and kept on a white t-shirt, a wife beater is what the humans called it. Which she never understood. His strong muscles rippled as he typed, and he occasionally stroked his beard, which caused a sensuous pool of lust to gather within the center of her thighs. She wondered what it would feel like if he were to stroke her skin that way....

Cassandra was jolted out of her thoughts, as she found him staring at her, with a cocky grin on his face. Blast the man! He'd caught her again!

Getting up from the bed, Cassandra decided to play it cool, now that she had her full strength again.

"I need to go out and hunt. Then when I return, we can start on this conversation that is gravely needed between us." She flung the words out, as if expecting no resistance. She was wrong.

"Hold up right there. Did you say hunt? If you think I'm about to let you go out and kill innocent people, and suck their blood like one of those bad tv vampires, you've got another thought coming, chick."

But Drago found he was talking to himself, within an empty room. She had vanished right before his eyes. Within thin air! He jumped out of the chair and cursed viciously.

"Shit! How the hell am I supposed to control a woman like that?" Drago dragged his frustrated hands over his short cut fade.

"The answer is, you don't idiot." He said out loud to himself, as he sat back down at the computer in acceptance. If there was anything Drago had learned, it was that you couldn't force a woman to do anything she didn't want to do willingly. No matter how powerful you were. It was better to catch bees with honey than with vinegar.

Focusing back on his task at hand, Drago reviewed the notes he'd made, and the reports of the missing men over the past ten years. There was nothing to tie them together. But he knew that there was a missing link. And he believed that he'd finally found it. All this time, and the past four years spent in that prison, had not been wasted. He would finally discover the cause of his brother's disappearance.

Drago sat back in the chair and twirled the pencil in his fingers, his mind racing back to that fateful day six years ago. When he had first learned that his brother Darren was missing.

He'd just gotten home from the military, and was honorably discharged for doing his time in the service. His brother was all he'd had left. And Drago knew he'd been into some trouble for a while. Getting into drugs, and mixing in with some really bad people. But he'd been hoping to turn him around. Get him some help, and possibly give him the support needed now that he was back home. But he'd been too late.

Drago clenched the pencil and it split in two, as he fought to keep his rage under control.

He had searched everywhere for almost a year with no luck. Everyone on the block where his brother had stayed, all said the same thing. He had vanished without a trace. No signs of forced entry, or evidence he had left. All of his things were still in the small apartment he shared with a roommate. The police of course knew nothing, and were not motivated to pursue the case of someone they considered a drug dealer, with a reputation a mile long.

Drago had taken matters into his own hands. And started an all out campaign to find his brother. He'd tried seeking the help of many non-profit organizations, but no one was willing to bother with his plight. Until suddenly, someone was. And that someone was the reason he'd landed in jail.

Drago pulled his thoughts back into the moment, and forced himself to focus. Everything he'd been through all came down to why he was here now. With this strange mysterious female, and following her to a place he was not certain he wanted to go. But he knew he had no choice.

He looked again at the PowerPoint he'd made on the computer, drawing a line between all of the locations where men had mysteriously vanished. Different cities, all spread out, and different male types. There was not one single thing to tie them all in together. Except the way they all disappeared. No trace. No evidence. And no further investigation.

But now that Drago had looked further, he believed he finally had a link. A small tie that could possibly bring all of these missing case victims together.

There was one thing he'd missed, and apparently so did all of law enforcement.

All of the missing men seemed to have had some sort of run in with the law, or an incident in their past that should have been brought up within the law, but wasn't. Every single missing man on the list for the past ten years, had in some way committed a crime.

They were all guilty men.

Chapter Nine

Cassandra waited in the shadows as she searched the night air for the dark souls she craved and hungered for. They were not hard to find. They were everywhere, and the lure to destroy them all was always begging for release.

But she had kept her vow and would not go back on her word now. Her people still needed her. And if she didn't hurry and get back to her mountains, her spirit sister would carry out her orders to the letter.

Cassandra felt her teeth extend and sharpen as she sensed a nearby pedestrian male, coming closer towards the alleyway she hid in. Her black glossy shoulder length curls glistened in the dark, and her clothes changed into a form fitting red dress. The neckline hanging low to expose her luscious butter cream breasts. She was seduction in the flesh, and her hips swayed slowly into the open, directly in the path of the approaching man.

The man was of average height, but overweight and chubby. His blood would fill her nicely without her being in danger of draining him.

The unsuspecting victim stopped dead in his tracks, at the sight of her. His eyes widened appreciatively, as he looked her up and down. He licked his lips suggestively, and quickly looked around to see if anyone else was nearby.

"Well, little lady. Looks like you're on the block tonight, huh? Looking for some company?"

The fat man smiled wickedly; his thoughts were clearly painted on his thick face. It was obvious he planned to take what he wanted. Whether she was willing to give it or not. Filthy disgusting human garbage! None of them deserved to live. None of them! She could see the darkness of his soul as if it was a moving mass of smoke within him. The feel of it caused the animal crave to rear its head within her. And she became crazed with it.

Cassandra bared her vicious fangs, and relished the instant fear that rose within the pathetic human's eyes. She latched onto him with preternatural speed, and knocked him onto the ground. His body collapsed with a ground shaking rumble, and she was on him immediately. Her teeth sinking into his neck and draining the blood from his body.

The man convulsed and jerked helplessly, as his eyes rolled to the back of his head. He was out, and almost dead before Cassandra yanked him away from her, in an anguished cry.

The man's body landed with a loud crash into the nearby dumpster. He would be completely weak, and have no memory of what had happened, but he was still alive. The wounds on his neck, she'd made sure to erase.

Cassandra stayed on the ground, leaning on her hands and knees. She panted as she fought to control the blood lust that was still within her. Each time, she seemed to come closer and closer to killing a human by draining their blood. Killing them outright was one thing. But if she killed them by the drainage of blood, she would turn completely into one of the empties. The vampire. And then, her people would be lost. Forever. She had to fight it.

Slowly, taking deep breaths, Cassandra drew herself back from the brink. She felt her blood begin to calm, and her skin returned to its normal caramel butter cream. Her eyes lost the red searing glow, and calmed back to the beautiful emerald green once again.

Cassandra sighed, and stood up. Snapping her fingers once, her clothes returned to the simple white V neck shirt, and black jeans. Her mind now centered and focused.

Now that she was fully fed, her thoughts went back to the human male she'd left alone in the hotel room. She'd begun to suspect he was holding back some things from her. Things she couldn't seem to penetrate his mind to discover. He had a lot to answer for, but she needed to find out more about him. And why she couldn't control or use certain powers against him. The main question she wanted answered was, how was it that she couldn't see the man's soul?

Tonight, she would get the answers she needed. And Drago was going to tell her all she wanted to know. Or she would be forced to use other means to make him do it.

***

She reappeared back into the room as if she'd never left, startling Drago and causing him to almost fling his knives through the air at her. He caught himself just in time, thankful that his instincts were extremely sharp. He glared at her.

"What the hell is wrong with you?! No one ever told you it's dangerous to sneak up on a man like that?" He thundered at her.

Cassandra merely smirked and shrugged her shoulders. Her gorgeous curls bouncing with the movement. She was secretly amused, because she had done it on purpose. She didn't know why, but it aroused her to no end to see him riled.

But it was not time for pleasantries or jokes. The clock was ticking, and they needed to get down to business.

"We need to talk, Drago. It's time we discussed a few things."

Drago noted the change in her tone, and calmly put away his knives. He agreed. Yes, it was high time they got a few things out into the open. She had to know what she was up against, and he needed to know more about who she was.

"Ok. Let's talk. You go first. Who are you, and why do you need me to go with you to this...Carpathian mountain? Why is it so important to you?"

Drago sat down at the desk, careful to remain away from her. Frankly, he just didn't trust himself to be too close to her right now. And he refused to examine the reasons why.

Cassandra sat down on the bed and made herself comfortable. The way she moved was like a sleek cat, her shapely thighs crossing each other, and her hips adjusting slowly onto the bed.

Drago's mouth watered as he watched her. He looked up at her face and saw that she was smiling knowingly at him. Damn it. Now it was his turn to blush. Drago cleared his throat and focused on the matter at hand.

"What I told you before was the truth." Cassandra began smoothly. "I need you to come with me. That is my job. Only, I've never had to explain it to anyone before now. Especially a human." She paused and looked at him, assessing how much she should tell this man. After all, he was only human. And human males could not be trusted. But so far, he'd saved her life twice. If he was really as bad as the others, why would he have done that? Wouldn't he have just raped and killed her, as all the dark souls were proven to do if given the chance?

Cassandra looked into his soft topaz and hazel green eyes. Pupils that were unlike any she'd ever seen on a man. In that moment, she made the call to trust him. A decision she was hoping to not regret.

"My people are dying, Drago. Starved and unable to procreate, we've grown very weak over the centuries. And need sustenance to survive."

"So what do you do to gain that sustenance?"

Drago asked the question with apprehension, not certain he wanted to know the answer.

Cassandra hesitated only a moment, then continued.

"My people have lived for a very long time. We come from an ancient culture of species that inhabited the earth, when what you call dinosaurs roamed this planet. This dates back to thousands of years ago. We were the first intelligent species, and we existed with the animals. There was an order to things. But then, mankind was discovered."

Cassandra tilted her head and folded her legs for the telling of her family history. It was a story she cherished, but one that also made her ache with pain. But she continued on, lost in her world of the Carpathian people.

"My people noticed that mankind was very different from us. Far less intelligent, weaker and more vulnerable. They didn't possess the abilities we had. They were like helpless insects crawling on the ground for every other living thing to prey on.

It was my ancestor, the great and honorable king of the Carpathians, king Loron, who decided to help the humans. They made an alliance with man to protect them from the great creatures that would feast on them. But there were some of the Carpathian people that did not agree with his decision."

Cassandra sighed and looked at her hands. Wishing that things had been different back then. But it wasn't.

"The king noticed that some of our people began to crave the human blood. It was sweeter, richer than the animal blood they were used to. Some began to hunt them, and it separated our people. Those that refused to conform to the king's rules were known as 'the empties.' What your kind now calls, the vampire."

Andrea Johnson

Drago sat up straighter, as she said the words he'd hoped not to hear. But it was confirmed. She was one of them.

"The empties began to grow in numbers, and so the king took the women of the Carpathians and hid them away beneath a heavily warded mountain. The Carpathian Mountains. He gave them seeds to continue to expand our population and grow. And it had worked...for a time."

Cassandra's voice trailed off sadly. Drago could see the pain in her face, and struggled with his warring emotions. He didn't know whether to feel sorry for her, or hate her.

"What happened? Why didn't the plan work? Why are your people dying, Cassandra?" Drago asked quietly.

Cassandra met his gaze and tried hard to hide the fury, but she couldn't.

"It was because of man, that's why. It didn't matter that the king had hidden away the women for safety, or given them seeds to reproduce. All of the remaining Carpathian males on earth were destroyed. Even the ones the women birthed and sent to the surface to join in the fight. They eventually never returned. Until there were no males left to provide seeds for the women. In time, there were only females left. And without sustenance, or seeds, they began to die off slowly. Until my queen made the decision to select a few chosen females that would venture to the surface. Each one would have only twenty years to find a human male that was special enough to help us procreate. She believed that it was possible. That perhaps humans had evolved enough to sustain our species. It was a very thin hope.

But for the past several centuries, each female chosen to search and find this one man had all failed. None of the men were suited to help us procreate. So now, I am the last of the chosen. There are no more after me. If I fail, the last of my remaining people will all die."

Cassandra grew silent, staring down at her hands. Drago didn't want to believe he'd seen the shine of tears.

"There was something you said earlier that struck me. What happened to all the Carpathian men? Why didn't they just stay down underneath the earth and protect their women? Why stay above surface if they were dying?"

Cassandra looked up at him as he asked the question, and the look within her emerald orbs gave Drago a deep feeling of trepidation.

"They stayed to protect the humans."

She said the words as if it were filled with venom.

"They stayed because they wanted to help mankind. To provide for them. To guard them. But man was fickle and petty, as he is now. The humans began to distrust the Carpathians as well as the empties. They could no longer separate the two, and saw them all as one and the same. They hunted them all down. Each and every one. It didn't matter if they were Carpathian or vampire. They were all annihilated. Brutally. Even the young men barely older than your teenagers. They found their resting places and burned the fields. The humans went on a war path, until there was not one of our kind left.

The only reason the women survived, is because they stayed underground. The humans never knew we were still there. Or we would've been destroyed as well. My people hid, for hundreds of years, scared, starving, and growing weaker. Until my queen had the bravery to give us something to hope for. A reason to fight to survive. So now here I am, trying to save my people any way I can, for the past eighteen years. But even I too have failed. So that is why I need you to come with me. To see if you can help us. I need to at least try, Drago."

Drago stared at her lovely face, and felt himself falling into something he knew he should not enter. But it was a losing battle.

"So if I go, and I'm not able to help you either, what happens to me? What happened to the men that all failed?"

There was a brief chilling moment of silence, as Cassandra looked down at her fingers. It was as if she suddenly couldn't look him in the eyes.

"They all went home. Just as you would, as well. If you cannot help us, then Drago, you too will be sent home...just as the others."

Chapter Ten

Drago contemplated everything he'd learned from Cassandra, and realized he'd suspected the truth all along. He'd known she was not like him; he just hadn't believed how completely different she was till now. She obviously wasn't a vampire, because she could still cast a reflection. But the sunlight could kill her. And she needed to drink blood to live.

She sat very still on the bed, lost in the thoughts of her world, and all of the pain that she no doubt must've endured. What must it be like to live life in darkness? To never be able to see the sun? Or to watch your loved ones perish all around you. Well he had a good idea of the latter.

Seeing her so small and still, touched something within him that was unfamiliar and strange. She had trusted him with her truth. And although he never would've believed her had he not seen her powers in full action, she still had given him the benefit of the doubt. The least he could do was comfort her.

Drago decided to ignore his better instincts, telling him to remain seated where he was, and went over to sit next to Cassandra on the bed.

At first he just sat there, their legs slightly brushing up against each other in a shared silence. But then, his hand began to move, and he gently lifted the curls away from her face. He softly used his fingers to raise her chin up a notch, so he could see her. And she could finally look at him.

He wanted her to see him. And desired to see her eyes just as they were in this moment. Filled with shiny tears she was fighting hard to hold back, and a pool of emerald crystals that were sparkling in her pupils from the emotion she was displaying.

Drago's breath was caught in his throat as he stared at the most beautiful vision he'd ever seen. And it wasn't just her physical that captured his senses. It was the undeniable vulnerability she was giving to him, even though it was clear she didn't want to.

Cursing silently, Drago crushed his mouth to her lips, and was immediately submerged within the depths of her kiss. Such luscious and sweet tasting honey, he was reveling in the fullness and texture.

Taking his tongue and exploring the satin insides of her skin.

Cassandra moaned helplessly, as Drago gently held onto her face, taking her lips as if he was sucking the soul from her body, if she ever had one.

Needing more of her now, unable to wait a moment longer, Drago removed her shirt, and feasted his large hands over her creamy soft globes.

Cassandra whimpered, shocked at the delicious ecstasy that was spiraling through her body at his possessive touch.

Drago twirled the taut nipples within his fingers, and then replaced it with his wet and hungry mouth. Cassandra reared back her head and cried out in pure joy, as he suckled and massaged her breasts, caressing them as if they were the most precious gift offered.

Never moving his mouth, Drago gently leaned her back onto the bed, loving the way her spine arched, as he suckled harder. Using his tongue, he trailed a moistened path down to the apex of her thighs, in which he paused to yank the jeans away from her hips. It was as if he hungered for her, and the fabric was his enemy.

Cassandra bucked in shock, her eyes turning a dark chocolate, as his lips and hands made contact with the soft skin in between her thighs. Trembling, she squirmed on the bed, opening her legs in invitation to the man who had so completely plundered her dark world.

Drago only paused to remove his t shirt and pants. He bent his head without hesitation and feasted on his buffet. Sinking into the warm and sweet liquid heat that beckoned to his very soul.

"Drago!" Cassandra shouted as she lost control and her fangs were now extended; she wasn't certain she could trust herself like this. She had always been in control. Always.

But Drago looked down at her, as he climbed on top of her and lifted her legs to receive him. He saw her fangs, but did not fear them. They strangely only turned him on further.

"Don't fight it, baby. Just trust me. Trust this. Just let go and let me guide you. I won't let you lose yourself; I've got you."

Drago paused as he stared into her eyes, as they changed color to a complete chocolate brown. She looked up at him, and breathed the words he yearned to hear. Needed to hear her say.

"I trust you, Drago."

He plunged deep. Delving into the heart of her with such passion, that he caught her cries within his lips, her squeals of pleasure lost within his ravaging tongue, as he took her savagely. Like a man that had lost all sense of himself and was clinging to the only thing that saved him.

Cassandra wrapped her legs around his strong muscular body, and let herself go. Moving in rhythm to his motion, and matching him passion for passion, as they plundered within the inner parts of their mind and body.

She reared back her head, her eyes turning a mixture of red and purple, as her teeth sharpened. Crying out in pure freedom, she plunged her teeth into his neck, to seal their union.

Drago was instantly filled with a sensuous heat unlike any he'd ever known. It was nothing like the first time she'd done it. This was entirely different. More erotic, and passionate.

Drago grunted in pleasure, as his eyes closed and he held her body close to his, stroking within her to the same motion her tongue was sucking his blood. Feeling a fulfillment that he'd never known existed.

Cassandra suckled his neck, as he pumped within her body, the complete high of his blood, mixed with the feel of his body connected to her, was more than she could take. Her eyes turned silver as she exploded in a climactic avalanche of passion. Drago released his seed inside of her, at the same time she was opening her mind to his.

Convulsing with pleasure, Cassandra shouted out something in her native language, as she lifted her head and squealed in ecstasy, his blood dripping from her lips, and his seed leaking from her thighs.

Drago crashed with her inside an emotional vortex of passion. Completely oblivious to anything as they climaxed together. Reaching the heights of an elevation where dimensions and other galaxies existed.

As they held each other, spinning within the maze of something that was more than either of them had anticipated, Drago was certain of only one thing.

Now that he had tasted what heaven was truly like, he was never going to return to earth. No matter what the price he had to pay to stay there.

Chapter Eleven

C.I.A. Headquarters, Langley, Virginia

Edward Beckman Jr, the head of the Counterintelligence Threat & Analytical Department, Reviewed the documents on his desk in quiet perusal. He switched from one file to the next, never saying a word, as he poured over all of the information that had been given to him. He didn't look up at the man that sat on the other side of his desk, waiting patiently for a response. As far as Edward was concerned, this was something that required great thought before he addressed the subject.

Finally, he closed the files and folded his hands across the desk. Making direct eye contact with the man who served as his lead analyst. The best information specialist he had in his department.

"Is this everything you can give me? Are you telling me that within these files, is all of the information we have so far on their whereabouts, and the target area you believe they're headed? You have nothing concrete, no solid evidence of the exact location?"

Edward spoke calmly to the man facing him, but the quiet tone was deceptive, and the man he directed the chilling words to, knew very well not to be fooled by it.

The man spoke up, clearing his throat as he knew what was coming next.

"Unfortunately, sir...the answer is yes."

The files were flung across the room in an instant fit of rage, as Edward leaped up and grabbed the man by the collar, his face scrunched in a mask of fury.

"How the hell could you lose them! You had one job, Bennet. Just one! And that was to keep track of Drago. It was all you had to do. Follow him, and report back to me. Once you knew he was with the woman, you were instructed to fall back. To keep out of the way and have your men just follow them. So tell me, Bennet, how is it that we have a speed chase through Waverly Virginia, over twenty people killed in an unusual explosion, and the media turning it all into a three ring circus!?"

The man known as Trevor James Bennet, was the lead analyst in the Counterintelligence Threat & Analytical Department, within the C.I.A. His reputation for solving the most diabolical cases, and gathering information within sources that were normally impossible to obtain, was unquestionable. His job was to keep tabs on anything remotely that constituted as a possible danger to the U.S. in terms of foreign technology instruments, and terrorists looking to infiltrate the country using sensitive information against them.

But this was a very special case. The type of files that were normally handled by those analysts located within area fifty one. It was not his expertise to assess something of this magnitude, but he had accepted the project and had been eager to please his boss, Edward Beckman JR. There was mention of a possible promotion if he succeeded in getting the information required.

But the problem was, it wasn't the first time they had lost track of Drago Brown. And when it had happened before, there had been hell to pay for it. But now he was back on the radar, and once again, they'd lost his trail. But this time it wasn't because of a mistake he'd made. This time, it was all because of Drago.

"Please sir, I know you're upset, but if you'd just give me another chance, I could fix this." Trevor, a short and slightly balding middle aged Caucasian man, pleaded with his boss.

But Edward, a largely built older Jewish man in his early sixties, was not willing to hear any excuses. He was nearing his retirement, and could not afford another scandal as they'd had to cover up several years ago.

"You're off the case, Bennet. I can't have another repeat of four years ago land on my desk again. We can't afford even a hint of foul play. Everyone within this department almost lost their jobs several years ago, and I am not going down for your callous loss of judgement!"

Edward shoved Bennet away from him in disgust. Turning and dragging his hand through his short salt and pepper hair. He walked over to the window, and looked out over the city. Regaining control of his composure, and fixing his suit back to its impeccable lines.

He contemplated this new dilemma, and reviewed his options. They had to work fast to recover from this recent mishap and somehow make the explosions appear to be accidental. Like a gas leak or something nearby. Anything to deflect the media away from the suspicious events in Waverly.

But in the meantime, he needed to put a new guy on Drago's trail. One that would be discreet and efficient. They needed to know where the woman's main hideout was, and if there were any others. And Drago would lead them directly to the prize he'd been searching for his entire career. They just had to find him first.

Locating Drago meant more to Edward than Bennet or anyone could understand. What Edward never disclosed to his department, was that the government had shut down the case four years ago. After the scandal had first broken out, and there were many questions no one could answer. And they had lost track of Drago. Without him, there had been nothing they could provide that would prove they still had a case. He had simply vanished from their tracking system. The government had ordered him to shut down the case, and pursue other files.

But Edward could not let it go. He had told his people that they would take a break, but never informed them the case was officially closed. He'd been hoping that one day he could resume searching. And then suddenly, only a few days ago, Drago Brown, known to the media as Jason Freeman, reappeared back on the map. But it was reported he'd been killed in route to the state prison, on his way to receive the death penalty.

Edward didn't know how that had all happened, but he knew for certain that Drago was not dead as the news reported him to be. He was too resourceful. Too stubborn. And so he'd dispatched Bennet and his men to trace him and follow him. And he was more than pleased to discover the woman that Drago was now traveling with. He suspected she was the answer to what he'd been searching for. The final piece in a puzzle he'd been putting together for years.

But Bennet had lost them. Foolishly ordering his men to apprehend them, when Drago had spotted the idiots tracking them. The rest was inevitable. But it also gave Edward the information he needed to make his next move. Now that he'd heard just what the woman could do, he could place his next plan into action. He just needed to find them first.

"Get me Stevens. I need him in here Asap. And tell no one about this." Edward ordered Bennet briskly, and the man eagerly nodded his head and left the office in a hurry.

Only too happy to put this in someone else's hands.

Edward stared out of the window silently. His hands in his pockets, and a look of finality on his chiseled face.

Stevens had men that were discreet indeed. Men who didn't ask questions, make mistakes, or perform foolish calls in judgement. They were good at blending in, and not being seen. Until it was time to do the job no one else wanted to do.

Yes. Stevens would know exactly who to call.

Chapter Twelve

They'd been driving for the past two nights in relative silence. Neither knowing what to say to each other, after having such an explosive encounter. It wasn't as if Drago hadn't had his share of women. He lost count of the ladies that had kept his mind off of things he didn't want to mention, while in the military. But there was never anyone who'd ever stayed with him. Or given him a reason to want anything from them. He never desired anything from anyone. Until now. Until Cassandra.

Cassandra remained silent and brooding, as they made their way into Texas. She couldn't begin to identify what was going on with her, but something was definitely different. Not only were her powers more heightened and...sensitive. She could feel him now in ways she couldn't before. But it wasn't like the other human men. She still could not see his soul. There was only a large void within him, like an open space where nothing existed. But now, she could see strange colors. Like a kaleidoscope, siphoning within the void. What was happening here? And why was she not able to control her emotions around him?

Cassandra leaned up in the car and stole a glance over at him. His powerful form was now clad in blue jeans, and a checkered shirt. His beard a little scraggly from the nonstop traveling. And his powerful muscular arms were exposed, as the sleeves were rolled up. Rippling in sinew as he held the wheel.

She felt her blood begin to do that boiling thing again, and quickly turned away from him. She was in unfamiliar territory, and didn't know how to handle this. He had fallen asleep next to her for a few hours, as she'd held him. She had actually held him in her arms, a thing that still shocked her senses. She'd gently trailed the roughness of his naked Adonis male body. Outlining every shape and hardened muscle. Memorizing the beauty of this strange and unique human male.

Cassandra watched the moving landscape as she realized that it was very possible she would have to destroy him. Just as she'd done with the others. But how could she perform her regular duties, when everything that she felt, had now seemed to shift and change?

Plus, she'd heard her spirit sister once again. The urgency was even thicker this time. Like a desperation. She couldn't tell him the full truth. Not all of it. If he knew what she'd done...Cassandra closed her eyes as a fresh wave of pain rose within her mind. She was somehow connected to him now. And though she still couldn't see everything, she knew that this was a very damaged and broken man. And if pushed, it could destroy more than just his mind.

Drago's curt voice interrupted her silent reverie, as he finally broke the monotony.

"We're in Texas now. So we need to go over the plan moving forward." Drago was all business now. He felt it was the best way to avoid any more discomfort and emotional baggage they seemed to be gathering. It was important that they remain focused, because the threat to both of them was still very real. And he had no doubt that they were still being hunted.

Cassandra, secretly pleased to hear him speak to her again, wisely hid her emotions this time, and blocked out all other thoughts clamoring in her head. He was right. Whoever was after them, seemed to want her desperately, and that led to a whole slew of questions he had yet to answer.

"I agree. But since you've decided to finally voice your opinion, don't you think it's time you told me exactly who is it that's after us, and why? I told you my side, but we never quite got around to you telling yours."

Cassandra left that sentence hanging in the air. Since both of them knew why they never did.

Drago cleared his throat, and easily deflected the question once again.

"Right now, it's not a matter of who is after us, you should be concerned with. It's how we're going to get out of the country alive."

Drago stayed focused on his driving as they steadily took the back roads and alternative routes he'd memorized. Since they needed to stay away from the major highways now, it had taken more time to get to the take off point where his guy was waiting for them. And he didn't like unplanned stops.

Cassandra glanced at him, she was wearing her hair up tonight in a ponytail, and it made her look seductively innocent and alluring. Drago tried not to look at her.

"Well you need to tell me something, Drago. Because how am I going to protect us, if the situation calls for it? Who is this guy we're meeting anyway?" She asked him in frustration.

"He was an old friend of mine in the military. We served on an outpost together in Israel, and he's one of the very few men in this world I trust."

He was the only man Drago trusted, since he'd lost his brother.

"He works at the Dallas Fort Worth Airport, in Texas, and carries cargo for the government on special errands. So he's able to move back and forth out of the country with ease. Customs never bother him. And he has a private jet plane that can take us safely out of the US. But we need to hurry, because he's scheduled to leave in twenty four hours, and he can't afford to delay his departure. The government would become suspicious, and that's the last thing he needs."

Drago frowned as he thought of the risk he was putting his older friend in. The man, known as Philip Crouch, was in his early fifties, but was more dependable than any other man he'd known. He had landed on his feet after they'd been discharged, even though it was almost impossible to find work for someone his age after leaving the service. But not Philip. He was a resilient man. And Drago hadn't wanted to drag him into this mess. But he'd had no other options.

Cassandra contemplated this new information, and looked at Drago in concern.

"What happens if we don't make it there in twenty four hours?" She asked him cautiously.

"He'd have to leave without us. And if that happens, we're screwed. Because we can't leave the country without tripping off some internal wire within the CIA. They would locate us instantly. Right now, they're watching every airport in every state, and have a man at each location trained to spot us and remain in the background. He could be the ticket attendant and we wouldn't know. And there's no one we can trust to keep our whereabouts hidden, without accepting some bribe to give us up."

"Except this man who served with you in Israel." Cassandra surmised quietly.

"Yes. And I will not put his life in danger. For anyone."

Drago replied in a clipped tone. Cassandra could see this man meant everything to him. And she wanted to make sure nothing happened to his friend as well.

She couldn't teleport with Drago for some reason, but she could still ensure their safety.

As if Drago picked up on her thoughts, he blurted out as an afterthought.

"And what do you mean, how are you going to protect us? Let's get one thing straight, little lady. I don't care how many powers you possess, or what your species can do. When you're with me, I will be doing the protecting. You got that? That's not up for debate."

Cassandra turned her face away and covered the smirk that curved her lips. It was so sweet. His need to protect her. Something no one had ever done, or could do before. She was more than happy to let him be her covering. But it was her yearning hope that he would prove to be so much more.

***

It took them more time than necessary to reach the port, because they had to stop at a hotel until dusk. So by the time they neared the scheduled check point, Drago was fanatic and anxious to see his friend. He was scheduled to take off within the hour, and so he hurried Casandra along, not wasting time on small talk.

Cassandra didn't need any assistance. She matched his pace, and was just as focused as he was. Her senses spanning out to scan the area for any possible threats. She needed to be ready.

Drago bypassed security, and headed for the secret entrance that Philip had given him access to. The airport was large, but he took them under the parking lot pathway, and entered a key to unlock a gate sectioned off as private.

Walking into a cleared runway, there was a small jet plane, sitting by itself in the darkened pathway. At first, it looked as if no one was there. It was too quiet, and Drago began to grow apprehensive.

Then all of a sudden, a tall man emerged from behind the plane, and stood there watching them. He didn't speak for a moment, and then stepped out of the shadows.

"Well it's about damn time you got here, you son of a bitch."

Chapter Thirteen

Drago broke into a wide grin, and Cassandra was floored to see how brilliant his smile could be. He chuckled and walked over to the man who was now approaching them with a lopsided smirk.

"It's been a long time, old man." Drago greeted his friend in a one armed hug, and it was a moment when they seemed to share an unspoken camaraderie. A bond that Cassandra knew he cherished.

Drago turned towards her with a nod, and gestured at the tall solidly built black man.

"Cassandra, I'd like you to meet my old friend, Philip Crouch. Philip, this is the woman I was telling you about, Cassandra. I'm helping her to get back home."

Cassandra found it slightly annoying that he'd introduced her as 'the woman I told you about.' She hid her disappointment well, and reached out her hand to shake Philip's.

But instead of taking hers in return, Philip simply stood and watched her. His eyes never leaving hers. Cassandra arched her brow, and stared right back at him. Her green eyes sparkling.

After an awkward moment, she lowered her hand. It was obvious he didn't like her.

Drago cleared his throat, to break the sudden tension in the air. The last thing he needed was for Cassandra to kill his friend with one of her fire balls.

"I think we should get moving, Philip. As I told you over the phone, they're tracking me. I don't know how many, or for how long. But I know he hasn't given up." Drago spoke briskly as Philip led them to the entrance of the plane.

Philip remained silent, as they all boarded the aircraft. He seemed a very mysterious man, bald with a grey lined goatee, and dressed in simple slacks and a blue shirt. He had an air of intelligence around him, as if he held a world of knowledge in his slightly wrinkled eyes. But he was a wise one, and kept his tongue when he needed to. Observing his environment and adapting as necessary.

He and Drago went back a long time, and had been through a lot. He was like a son to him, and he wouldn't let anything happen to that man.

So that was why when he took one look at the woman Drago had with him, he'd known his dear friend was in deep. She had a look about her. A very dangerous presence indeed. He had a way of sensing things in people. It was part of what helped him to survive in the military. He could almost see into a person's heart. Could feel their vibe. But for some strange reason, there was nothing where this woman was concerned. It was as if she was an empty shell inside. Philip was prepared to take Drago aside and inform him he wasn't going anywhere with this woman. There was something seriously wrong with her.

But then, he had seen the way she looked at Drago. And his assessment of her changed drastically. She may be surrounded by trouble and darkness, but when she looked at his boy, there was light in her eyes that shone as if she was a beacon. It was unguarded, and she probably didn't realize he could see it. But this woman truly cared for Drago.

And that was enough for Philip.

He still didn't want to shake her hand though. Too many bad vibes, and he wanted no remnants of her shadows touching him.

Cassandra made herself comfortable in one of the seats in the back, as they began to take off. While Drago sat in the front next to his weird friend. It hadn't escaped her notice that he didn't like her. She could see inside of him. He was one she definitely would've seduced and brought into the gate. He had a dark past, and she could see his soul. But now, there was an oddity she couldn't quite place.

Before, all she could see was darkness within a man's soul. All of the bad things he'd done, and the misdeeds that she used to bring judgement down on them swiftly. But ever since she and Drago had mated, there was something different about her sight, when peering into a man's soul. The darkness was still there, a huge black vapor like mist that lived within the human, and shadowed his aura. But recently, she started seeing other things. Different shades of color within the black. Some had purple, or green, shades of grey, or blue and red. There were some that had bursts of color like rainbows, filtering all throughout the darkness. It was confusing, and

Cassandra was dumbfounded. She didn't know what it all meant. She had never been trained to see anything else but the darkness.

She sat back and leaned her head on the seat, pondering these latest developments. Could it be that they had been searching for the wrong thing? Did she and her Carpathian sisters confuse the message the queen had given them, and was making a fatal mistake?

Cassandra's blood raced in her veins, as she used the cup to drink the sustenance, she had drained from a cow earlier. Another concession she was making for Drago. She was changing. In ways she couldn't yet understand. And none of it made sense. All she knew is that it had something to do with Drago, and she needed to get him to the gate before it was too late. Because now that she'd mated with him, she couldn't seem to communicate with her spirit sister at all. She could only feel her, but not reach her. And that was a problem.

Cassandra closed her eyes, and could only hope they made it to the mountains in time.

***

Drago went in and checked on Cassandra. Now that it was dawn, he wanted to make certain the windows were all closed, and that she was safe.

He found her sprawled out way in the back, laying across two sweats. Her legs were curled up under her, and she had her arms folded up to her face, in the fetal position. Drago watched her, as she slept the healing sleep of her people. It was unnerving, because she had no pulse, and she looked dead. But at the same time, she was the most beautiful thing he'd ever seen.

Taking a blanket from the above compartment, he placed it over her gently. Touching the softness of her cheeks as he did so. His heart lurched at the gentle slope of her neck, and elegant swell of her breasts. He didn't know how it happened, or exactly why. But somehow, he had fallen head over heels in love with this unusual creature. She wasn't even human, but he didn't care. He would do anything to protect her. Anything.

Drago took another look at her, and then walked back to the front. He sat down next to Philip in the co-pilot's seat, and tried not to think about what he'd just discovered about his newfound feelings for Cassandra.

"Man, you really are gone."

Philip said with a straight face, continuing to look on at the control panel. He took one look at Drago, and knew his friend was completely sunk.

"It wasn't supposed to happen this way, Philip."

Drago began with resignation. He knew he could never lie to his old friend. He looked out over the clouds and the rising sun. A beautiful display she would never be able to witness. How could he ever make it work? He had no idea what he was doing anymore, and that scared him more than anything.

"Let's be real, son. Love never happens as it's supposed to. I can vouch for that! But it's what you do with it once you have it, that matters in the long run." Philip glanced over at him curiously.

"Have you told her yet?"

Drago tensed in his seat, and his jaw clenched. He knew exactly what Philip was referring to, and he didn't want to face it. Not yet. He wanted to pretend that things could be good for them, even for a moment. Just to feel as if he didn't have to run anymore.

"I can't, Philip. She would never have me, if she knew the truth. If she knew just what type of man I really am."

"What the hell are you doing, Drago? You didn't learn anything at all while we were locked away in those POW camps? Nothing about what happens to a man when he buries things too long? If she's what you want, then you gotta tell her, man. And if she can't handle it, then she wasn't meant for you. There's no in between when it comes to love. It's all, or nothing at all."

Philip always gave it to him straight. He never sugar coated the truth. Always dropped it on him like a ton of bricks. And Drago always appreciated him for that. Just not today.

"I need to handle this my way, ok? You don't understand everything involved with this girl. She told me some things that...I'm not even sure how to process. And she says she needs my help. So I'm going to do everything I can to be there for her."

Drago was adamant, and refused to hear what his friend was saying.

Philip shook his head as he looked at him.

"Come on son, you're smarter than that! You know how these things can go for men like us. If you think you have a real chance with this woman, tell her the truth. Let her decide. Because if not, it will come out either way. And you may not be able to handle the repercussions."

Drago clenched his teeth and withdrew into himself. Not saying anything further. Philip didn't understand. He just couldn't lose Cassandra. She was an existence within his empty void of darkness. She made him feel. Believe. He hadn't wanted to. But he did. But he wasn't ready to tell her how he felt, or share the secrets that may tear her away from him forever. He wanted to wait a bit longer. And just...experience what it felt to be in love.

Philip cursed silently, and knew it was pointless. Drago was in over his head. And the fool would not listen to reason. There was nothing he could do, but give him the support he needed and pray that it all turned out well.

Because if the people following him were the same ones that caused him to land in prison on death row, Philip knew his friend was headed for more than just trouble.

Chapter Fourteen

Catalina had made it to the surface, after waiting several more days for a signal from Cassandra. She'd finally realized she would have to venture out, and perform the task her spirit sister had urged her to do. But now there was a bigger threat at hand.

Catalina could not ignore the fact that she'd seen one of their own violate a sacred oath. They were not supposed to drink human blood. The temptation was too high. The gate keepers were the ones who were supposed to bring them sustenance. But Cassandra had been gone too long. And the women were beginning to grow restless. Was it possible some of them had even gone to the surface? Why was it so easy for one of the elected judge of man, to take his blood and place it in a bottle for preservation?

There were too many unanswered questions, and with Cassandra not communicating, she'd had to make a decision.

Before Catalina traveled to the surface, she needed more evidence. She had to see what the judge would do with the bottle of blood.

So she had turned around, and followed the trace of the Carpathian female back to their home base. An underground world of darkness.

Over the centuries, the underground caves had grown larger, to make room for the expanding population. They all had assigned tasks, and roles. The gate keepers were the most highly revered of the women. They were the guardians of their world, and tasked with protecting them, and finding their food supplies every night.

Then there were the builders. The women who made sure their cave homes were maintained, and didn't collapse in on them. The replenishers came next. These women were assigned as life savers to those who had grown too weak on nourishment. They provided their own blood to be shared when needed, and often sacrificed themselves for others. A replenisher had to have very strong blood, and could not mingle with others or use her energy too freely. She was basically a refrigerator, waiting to be used when needed. It was the least desirable position anyone wanted. But those selected took it with honor. And then there was the crystal makers. In which Catalina was one of them. These were women that found crystals within the diamonds found in the cave, and used them to make things with. Their bedding, clothing, even furniture came from the crystals. Most of the Carpathian women were crystal makers. They would be in the deeper mines all night long, until it was time to take their rest. It was all they did. Find them, and make supplies from them.

But it was the judges, and the order who ran things among their people. The judges, and gate keepers were all chosen by the women that ran the order. There was always six Carpathian women that resided on the board. And if one of them died, there was a lengthy process for a replacement.

Catalina walked within the dimly lit pathways, and headed for the entrance of the women for the order. A line that came from the queen Besilia herself.

She needed to know if anything had changed, but she must be discreet. If there was anarchy afoot, she did not want to tip her hand too soon.

Catalina had gone and approached the narrow doorway which led to a wide opening with stones and pillars that held separate entrances and chambers. In the center was a large platform, and a long crystal glass table with six chairs. The women were already seated within them. All speaking to each other in quiet whispers. It was the ancient Carpathian women's way. To be quiet and docile unless force was needed. A tradition some of the younger women didn't keep.

But even though they whispered, she could hear every word. Her heightened senses even stronger with the elixir Cassandra had given her. What she'd overheard had chilled her bones.

"We are out of time and options, Bruna. What choice do we have? We have to begin rounding up the human men, and bringing them to us. We can no longer just sit down here and watch each other die!" The female on the end spoke up. Her silver white hair pulled back to reveal a pale and chalky face.

"If we do that, then we are forfeiting our right to the queen's legacy, Simone. We cannot order the annihilation of man. The same thing will happen to us, as happened to our men all those centuries ago. We must be wise." The one called Bruna, a beautiful and chocolate toned brunette responded.

"We will also be dead." Another one spoke up in defense of Simone. She had long red hair and smooth peach colored skin. Her yellow eyes shone in anger.

"How long have we waited, Bruna? For centuries! Our women starve, and though the queen was wise, she could not see how all this would turn out."

"Tiana is right, Bruna." A fourth woman spoke up, she had caramel colored skin, and long wavy black hair. Her silver eyes were sad but resigned.

"Even the queen had said if we couldn't find the one to help us, we should destroy them all. That was her proclamation. I feel we have waited enough."

A fifth woman spoke up in defense of Bruna, and held up her hand. She had light creamy skin, and blue crystal eyes. Her hair was salt and pepper, and she spoke with frustration.

"If we do this, we lose our self to the human way. It could all end up bad for us. We cannot just give up hope, ladies!"

But it was the sixth woman, the one who sat in the center that held up a hand for silence. She wore her hair in elegant black curls on top of her head, and her smooth brown skin showcased eyes of lavender and blue. It was Mariella. The head of the order, and the only living descendant of the queen.

"We will not be divided on this, ladies. We are Carpathians. We are not like those animals that live above us. We've already made the decision to use the judges to slowly start feeding the women blood, from the human men the gate keepers capture. But now, what we are discussing is far more dangerous, and requires some thought. If we travel above ground, we will be waging war. And the humans will know we exist. We won't be able to go back from that. Once that line is crossed, it is done. So we must make this decision carefully. Our last gate keeper has not returned with another male. So we must choose. We will vote on what should be done. And then we will decide. But whatever the outcome, we must do it quickly. We are out of time."

Catalina now stood alone looking down at the glistening lake of Morskie, Oko. Cassandra was nowhere to be found, and her people were getting ready to make war on the human population. She could no longer wait. It was up to her.

Taking a deep breath, she reveled at the beauty of the world for the first time. The brilliant stars in the immense and perfect sky. But unfortunately, she could not enjoy it. Catalina began to walk towards the lake, needing the elements of the water to create the first part of plan one.

Chapter Fifteen

"They were located, sir. Boarding a carrier jet plane in the DFW airport. The pilot is a retired military veteran. Philip Crouch. He's a cargo placement and receiver for the unites states government, and is on route to Paris France for a weapons installment delivery, for a special unit assigned there."

Edward Beckman Jr. listened as the report was given to him. He sat inside one of the smaller conference rooms, and held the cell phone to his ear. It was important that discretion was used at all times when dealing with something of this magnitude. So using a company phone, or even meeting with the guy Stevens hired, was risky. It was best if they never met face to face. This way, if he needed to order the man terminated for loose ends, the job would be easier to do. And there would be no ties leading back to him. The phone he was using was a disposable one. Untraceable once the chip was removed. A gift from the department for more classified assignments.

"You did good. Are you certain they never saw you? It's important that you remain undetected at all times, until we know their final destination."

The raspy voice on the other replied curtly.

"I know how to do my job. The one you call Drago is smart. I noticed him checking for backdrops. People within the crowds, and scanning entries and exits. He's a sharp one. But not keen enough. If he thought I was there, they would've changed plans. No. He's oblivious to me."

"And what about the woman? Were there any details about her you noticed? Did she do anything out of the ordinary?"

"Other than the fact that she's a walking sex bomb?" The man on the phone chuckled sarcastically, and Edward frowned with impatience.

"I need answers. Don't waste my time or my money. Or you will find yourself just another casualty of the US government." Edward replied smoothly. Earning an immediate silence on the other end.

"If they are going to Paris, France to drop off cargo, I need them followed. I want to know if that's the only place they're headed. I need armed men who are already there, ready to apprehend them if necessary. Can you do this?" Edward bit out in an annoyed tone.

There was a slight pause on the phone, and then a quiet but firm reply.

"I can do anything I'm being paid for. Just make sure that money keeps coming, and so will the information. I'll let you know once they land. And you can let me know what you want to do with them from there."

Edward clenched the phone a little harder, as he looked down at the photo sent to him from the guy. It was on the conference table in front of him. Only of Drago and the pilot, Philip Crouch. There was nothing next to Drago except a grey blurry fog like form. The spot which he knew the woman must have been standing. It was believed she could cast reflection, but not in photos or video cameras. How interesting.

He held the photo in his hand, and his eyes narrowed further. It was her. He knew it was the one he was looking for.

"Just wait for my signal. We will need the specialists to handle this one. Make sure they're already there in France. Waiting for them."

* * *

The entire flight was a ten hour trip from Dallas Texas, to Philip's cargo drop off point in Paris, France. He had enough fuel to make it for the full journey to France. But would have to refuel there, for the remaining hour flight into Poland.

Drago was careful to watch over Cassandra for the first few hours, as they crossed over the Atlantic Ocean, leaving a rising sun to pass into one that was only just setting. It was fascinating, actually. To witness the effect of the different time zones within her face and body.

Cassandra slept like the dead for the first four hours, her face pale and cold as glass. Her skin had changed from its normal lustrous butter cream tone, to a pale and bland milky white. Looking as if she was an indoor mannequin, a lifeless display sprawled on the two seats.

But Drago had seen her change into this before, plenty of times while they traveled together. It was like her body went through a complete metamorphosis once the sun had risen. If she wasn't vampire, then what manner of species was this? That could not be exposed to the sun? Was it some form of highly evolved reverse plant syndrome chemical? Drago pondered this a time or two, as he'd watched her change from life to a death like sleep. There was a lot he'd learned while in the military, about chemicals and elements that could kill you instantly.

He wondered if Cassandra had an aversion to light, just as plants wilted and died if prevented from feeling the rays of the sun. It was interesting. And he yearned to find out more about her, who she was, and how he could save her.

Drago watched her now, as her body adjusted to the new time zone. She was adapting to the change in climate swiftly, and he was amazed, as her body started to change color before his eyes. Going from pale ghost, back to the beautiful creamy glow he'd grown accustomed to. Even though it hadn't been a full night, her eyes opened up and stared into his, the sparkling emerald green luminescence more breath taking than ever.

Cassandra watched him for a moment, feeling a completion of pure peace, seeing him there looking at her. Protecting her as she slept. It took her a moment to gather her wits.

"Were you watching over me the whole time?"

She spoke in a sultry and low voice, which had the immediate results of making him rise to the occasion.

Drago smirked, as he brushed a wayward curl from her cheek.

"Only so we could talk. We need to discuss the plan once we land in...your Carpathian Mountains." Drago brought it back to the main subject at hand. He had to remain focused, and find out exactly what needed to be done to help her and her people.

Cassandra suddenly stiffened at the mention of her home, and moved her legs off of him to sit up.

She dragged a hand through her disarrayed curls, trying to give herself a second to respond.

"Yes, we need to go over some things. I never did thank you for agreeing to come with me. The fact that you're willing to help me is more than any human has ever done for me."

Of course, it was due to the fact that Cassandra had never given them a choice before. If she saw their human soul was black, she immediately took them. And then they were placed before one of the judges. And if found guilty, which all of them were, they were killed slowly, and painfully. Sometimes over days and weeks.

Cassandra quickly removed her thoughts from those dark memories. The thought of Drago going through what those men had encountered...she could not bear it if something were to happen to him. She just couldn't.

"Of course I will. But first, I need to understand exactly what is needed to help you. I'm not sure how I can do that. Is it my blood you need? I mean...you never explained how one human man could help you procreate your species. And if all the others failed, how do you know I won't also? Is it like some sort of sex thing, where I have to sleep with all your women? Cause that would be interesting." Drago chuckled at his own joke, highly intrigued at the thought.

Cassandra glared at him, her eyes turning swiftly from green to blazing red. She stared at him with a lethal and hungry force. The thought of him even going near one of the other women, set her blood on fire. Suddenly she was outrageously jealous, like a female wolf guarding her territory. Drago's humor withered and died instantly at the sight of her fury.

"Woah, ok calm down Cassandra. I was just joking. It was just a little humor ok? Sheesh. I didn't mean anything by it. Honestly."

Cassandra fought for control, and slowly her eyes returned to their normal color. Her expanding fangs, retreated, and went away. Turning towards the window, she moved slightly away from him to give herself some space.

It worried her. This reaction to him and her lack of control. She didn't know how to handle it.

"I'm sorry Cassandra. I shouldn't've said that. It was stupid and a real dumb ass thing to say. I apologize. But I really do need to know what we're dealing with here. You have to let me know how I can help you." Drago's voice trailed off.

Cassandra stared out of the window, as they passed over the Atlantic Ocean. The setting sun casting a purplish streak across the skyline. She was lost in thought when suddenly she felt a ripple within her body. It was subtle. But still strong enough that she could feel it all over her skin. It was deep and resonating, and lifted the hairs on the back of her head.

Cassandra closed her eyes without giving away anything to Drago. She began to focus her mind and reach out with her senses. It was the Carpathian call of her spirit sister. She was communicating in another way, because they were somehow being blocked. They could not talk to each other any longer, and Cassandra believed it had something to do with her mating with Drago. An act that was forbidden, unless he had been judged worthy.

Cassandra opened her mind, and tried to see what her sister was saying, but could only feel an urgency and fear. There were images that were flashing in her mind. The order. A bottle of human blood. The night skies, and.... then the connection was cut. Suddenly there was nothing, only a deepening sense of despair and terror.

Cassandra's eyes flashed open in panic and fear. Something was terribly wrong. Her sister had been headed to the lake. But there was something going on within the mountains. She had to get there. This was all her fault. While she'd been cavorting around in the bed, and flirting with a human stranger, her spirit sister was now exposed to the outside world. A danger she wouldn't be in, had Cassandra been back in time.

Feeling a hardening within her mind, Cassandra resolved that getting to Catalina and her people was the only thing that mattered now. Drago was just a human man. Nothing more. Her mission first and foremost must always be to her people. And if that meant sacrificing Drago, then so be it. She'd done it thousands of times before. It was her job. If necessary, she would do it again. But she needed him on her side till then.

Regaining her composure, Cassandra smiled and turned back to face him. Her words were chosen carefully this time.

"Listen, don't worry about how you'll help us. The most important thing is that you're willing to try. We'll go there, and the rest will take care of itself."

Cassandra smiled gently at him, to reassure him and make him comfortable. But oddly, Drago noticed that this time the smile never quite reached her eyes.

Chapter Sixteen

Paris, France

They landed close to ten in the evening, and Philip gave them swift instructions before they left the plane.

"I only have one hour to unload and meet with the delivery drop off official. It never takes me longer than that. My suggestion is that you two lay low at this nearby boarding house over in Paris. I know the lady who runs it, and she's loyal to me, cause I help fund her business."

Philip gave a lopsided grin, before moving on.

"Anyway, she knows you're coming. But don't interact with the people. Strangers have a way of making headline news the next day, if you know what I mean." Philip gave Drago a piece of paper with written directions of the address, and the lady's name.

"I have a car parked here in the port garage. Here are the keys. Go there, stay put in the room, and then meet me back here at exactly eleven. If you're not back here by eleven, Drago…. I'll have to leave without you. You understand what I'm saying right?"

Drago nodded his head at his old friend, understanding completely. He wouldn't put his comrade in more danger by blowing his cover. The Paris government had given him clemency. But if he lingered past his time, all deals were forfeited.

"I understand Philip. We'll be here. Go and handle your business and don't worry about us. We'll be fine." Drago took Cassandra's hand and started to lead her away.

Cassandra looked back towards Philip as they left him by the plane. And the expression in his eyes as he watched her, said it all.

He still didn't trust her. And the fact that he was right not to, was more unnerving for her than she cared to admit.

***

Drago drove them to the location without mishap. The ride was a silent one, as Cassandra seemed to be in a brooding mood ever since their talk on the plane. It was as if she had distanced herself from him. And it was hard to reach her.

At first, he felt maybe it was for the best. He still wasn't certain if he could even help her. But as they arrived at the one story boarding house settled deep within a rural part of the woods, he was beginning to think it was the worst idea he could imagine.

Cassandra followed Drago's lead, as they walked up to a small cottage looking structure. There was something about the place that struck her as odd. It was very quiet, even for the late hour. The house was situated in the center of a large clearing, a freshly mowed lawn was on both sides of a driveway, that neatly circled and led straight up to the house. It was well kept up, with white shingles and flowerpots in the front windows.

Everything was picture perfect. Almost too perfect, and Cassandra's senses began to go on the alert. There was no apparent danger, but it was clear that something was not right.

"Drago, I don't like this place. It's too quiet. It doesn't feel right."

Cassandra squeezed his hand, and urged him to listen to her. The surrounding trees were too still.

Drago frowned as he looked at her. Confused that she would feel apprehension towards anything. Philip would never send them anywhere that wasn't airtight. And besides, he didn't detect anything unusual or sinister. And his instincts were almost always on point.

"Look, it's only going to be for about forty five minutes now. We've had a long flight, and I know you need to feed. Let's get inside and figure out how we can get you some...sustenance."

Cassandra did need to regenerate her energy. She hadn't fed on the plane, since she'd awakened. And they didn't have time to find any replacements for her before leaving. What he said made sense. And even though her skin was still prickling that danger was near, she nodded her head, as she felt the aching need of hunger begin to overshadow her concerns.

They walked up to the door and Drago knocked firmly. Taking a few steps back as a precautionary method. They didn't have long to wait.

The door was opened by a short and plump woman. She was fairly attractive, looked to be in her late forties, with a round cheerful face and big brown eyes. She wore her hair in a tight bun, and was draped in a cotton dress with an apron around it. She smiled looking directly at Drago, a recognition lighting up her eyes.

"You're here. I was expecting you, bonsoir."

She ushered them in quickly. Cassandra noted that the woman very subtlety scanned the outside trees, as they entered in. She quickly closed the door behind them.

"I know you don't have much time, but I make your stay here comfortable, comprendre? I have made two rooms for you as Phillipe requested. I already put food for you in there, oui? So please, let me know if you need anything at all. My name is Adele."

She spoke quickly, her heavily accented English mixing with her French. Adele guided them through a large living area, that was beautifully furnished. A fireplace stood in the middle as the showpiece, and a coffee table and sofa were comfortably arranged to the side. Magazines were piled on an end table, and a flat screen TV was hung on a wall for viewers.

It was a very cozy setting for a boarding house. And would have been very inviting. Except for the fact that they were the only other occupants in the house.

Cassandra could not sense any other humans within the dwelling. Sleeping or awake. Based on what Philip indicated, the business was a thriving one. So where were all the other boarders?

Cassandra decided to keep her thoughts to herself, as they were led down a hall. Adele showed the first room to Drago, smiling at him very flirtatiously.

"This is your room, monsieur Drago. Please let me know if there is anything you...need."

She touched his shoulder suggestively. Drago smiled politely, and looked over at Cassandra.

She was not smiling.

"And this is your room, madame." Adele took Cassandra further down the hall, separating her from Drago. Cassandra frowned and paused, looking back at him.

"I thought our rooms would be closer together?" She asked their hostess, not liking the situation at all.

Adele smiled, but Cassandra noticed that she wasn't as cheerful when she first opened the door.

"Oh no, madame. We do not put single strangers too close together. It is not...how you say...appropriate, oui?"

"I don't give a shit about your fucking rules, oui? Put me and my partner closer together or I'll cut your fucking head off, oui?"

Cassandra replied back very smoothly, mocking Adele, never breaking eye contact. She spoke quietly so Drago wouldn't hear, but with enough venom in her voice to make the threat a real one.

Adele stuttered, a look of shock and fear rising within her eyes. Good. Cassandra wanted the simpering woman to be afraid. She didn't like her, and felt her whole cheerful greeting was a sham. It gave her deep satisfaction to see her rush to comply, and immediately lead her back down the hall to the room next to Drago's.

Drago frowned as he opened his door, looking up to see Cassandra coming back to the room next to his. He watched as Adele rushed away, her head lowered and avoiding eye contact with them again.

He sighed and looked back at Cassandra as she opened her door.

"What did you do to her, Cassandra? We have to keep a low profile, remember? We don't want to do anything that could draw the attention."

Cassandra shrugged her slender shoulders in innocence, and tossed her mane of curls to the side, giving Drago a rush of heat within the pit of his stomach.

"I have no idea what you're talking about, monsieur." Cassandra batted her eyes and mocked Adele's accent, as she entered her room and closed the door behind her. She could hear Drago's laughter in the hall as it faded.

Cassandra smiled to herself, loving the sound of his laughter, but then quickly refocused her thoughts.

The room was simple in design. A single bed lined the wall, next to a plain brown dresser. There was one chair in the room, a very small closet, and a window that was draped in a sheer white curtain. The walls were bare, and so was the floor. No carpet. All though the rest of the house was. She wondered if Drago's room was the same.

Going to the bed, she sat down and contemplated how she would hunt. This was unfamiliar territory, but then again, that never mattered to her before. It seemed that since she'd gotten with Drago, she was more concerned about details that never made a difference before.

It would have been nice to feast on the foolish Adele woman, but she knew that was out of the question.

Cassandra lowered her head and made herself grow still. She needed to focus her energy on finding nearby replenishment. And she needed to do it quickly. They could not be late for the return to the plane.

She closed her eyes and opened her mind. Her energy reaching out to all corners within a two mile radius of their location. Searching for human male prey with dark souls.

But she didn't get very far.

They were good. So good that they had gone undetected by her all this time. How was that even possible? Like they had known how to hide from her. Slowing their heartbeats to an almost imperceptible rhythm.

Even as Cassandra sensed the two dozen men closing in on the cottage, she felt her skin punctured by something sharp. Her body stiffened in cold pain.

Opening her eyes, she saw a strange looking dart embedded within her chest. It was laced with something peppered all over the surface. She couldn't identify it, but it had the ability to paralyze her instantly.

She fell to the floor in limp shock, just as the intruders began to raid the house.

Chapter Seventeen

Drago placed his black box onto the bed and sat down. He needed to figure something out, and quick. Even though he'd told Cassandra everything was fine, he had sensed something too. Deep in his gut after they had entered the house, and the woman called Adele had looked outside. Why did she seem so nervous? Was she expecting someone else? And where were the other boarders Philip told him would be there?

Drago had lived long enough to know when something was up. But alerting Cassandra to it at the moment would not have been wise. She tended to be a bit hotheaded at times, and might have killed the woman out of spite.

Opening the box, he retrieved his knives, and handgun. Something he hadn't wanted Philip to see. There would have been too many questions he didn't feel like answering.

Not knowing exactly how many were out there, or when they would strike, he had to come up with an exit plan. And he believed he knew the only one that would work. Cassandra.

She hadn't fed as yet. If they worked together, they could take out every single one of them, and still be in time for the return flight.

Just as Drago was closing the box, he heard a loud thump in the room Cassandra was in. at the same time the front door caved in with a swarm of men.

Going into high stealth mode, Drago immediately grabbed his box and jumped into action. Crashing out of his room and slamming into Cassandra's. He found her laying on the floor, her eyes wide open, as she convulsed with an object sticking out of her chest.

"Shit!"

Drago ran to the bed and threw the mattress off, moving the frame to block the door from entry. They were locked in, but it would buy them a few precious moments. He raced over and knelt down beside Cassandra, lifting her face from the floor.

"Baby, what did they do to you? What is this?"

Drago was filled with rage, as he stared at her, her face contorted with pain. He carefully pulled the dart out of her chest, leaving a gaping bleeding hole, that pooled down her body.

Cassandra's eyes rolled into her head, and she began to tremble even harder. Her body beginning to steam and bubble.

"What the fuck! Cassandra, baby tell me how to help you! You gotta fight this shit. I won't let you go down like this." Drago felt the helpless fury as he looked at her, hearing the men getting closer, checking every room. He couldn't lose her. If he had only listened to her when she'd told them not to enter the place, she wouldn't be dying right now. This was all his fault.

Drago balled his fists, and readied his gun. If this was the way it would be, he would go out guns blazing. But he would not leave her like this. He would do for her what he should have done first, before they even got there. He would replenish her.

Taking his knife, Drago sliced his flesh open on his chest, and lifted her convulsing head to his wound. It was hard to keep her still as she was shaking so violently, but he guided her moving mouth to his blood, hoping she could feed.

He could hear the men were almost upon them. The crashing sounds of the spray of bullets and furniture were getting closer, when suddenly a blinding pain slashed through his skin.

He cried out in surprise and agony, as he looked down to see that Cassandra had latched onto him. But her eyes were blood red and glowing. Her nails were distended, and her face had changed. She looked evil and deadly. She was sucking the life out of him, at hyper speed. Faster than she'd ever done before.

"Cassandra, wait…it's too fast…too much!" Drago held her head, as she continued to draw from him. Regardless of the fact that she was draining him, he couldn't stop her. He had to give her what she needed. Even if that meant all of him.

Drago felt the room spin as the door was sprayed with bullets. The frame being splintered into pieces as it was crashed to the side, a slew of men charging in at them.

He could only be thankful that he had given to Cassandra the last of him, just as he stared down the barrel of death.

***

Cassandra felt the rush of life propelled back into her, and flung Drago away, just before she took his completely. Even as she turned and shielded him from the bullet that was aimed at his head. Her hand blocked the targeted darts as they came at her, to try and paralyze her once more. She stood up slowly, her eyes blazing red and her skin glowing in flames, as she stared at them tauntingly.

"You boys have got to do better than that. Did you really think you could catch me twice?"

Cassandra smiled and revealed her sharp fangs.

"Your weapons are no longer useful to you."

Shouting, the men began to shoot at her with full force, firing their guns and emptying their clips with everything they had.

Cassandra used her speed to shield Drago, creating a force field of power that deflected all of the bullets. The shells fell helplessly to the ground around them. Until none of the men had any ammunition left. They stood in wide eyed fear, as they watched her. She stood still and smiled. Cocking her head.

"Now...it's my turn."

Cassandra hissed as she flew into the air at them faster than their eyes could see.

The men screamed in terror, racing out of the room and trying to escape the house.

She latched onto them one by one, not feeding, just simply killing them all. Severing their heads with her nails as she leaped from one body to the next.

They ran out into the hall like ants, scattering in their panic. Cassandra leaped onto the wall, and galloped on the side like an animal, falling onto them and castrating their heads. Her teeth were like knives, as she swiped the flesh of each man, and used her nails to shatter open their bodies. Splitting some of them in half, and flinging the flesh against the walls like discarded chicken bones.

There was blood everywhere. Pools of it lined the hall and floors, and the living area was now littered with carcasses and chopped up flesh.

Cassandra stood in the aftermath; her body covered in blood from head to toe. Licking some of it from her fingers calmly. Now she could see why the empties enjoyed this so much. Had she killed them by drinking their blood, she would be full vampire by now. And no human around her would be safe. Not even Drago.

Drago.

Cassandra rushed back into the room, climbing over the sea of bodies, to find him still on the floor, surrounded by blood and gore from the battle. He was still knocked out. Almost fully drained from her feeding off him.

Her emotions suddenly all came crashing down on her at once, as she collapsed to her knees next to him. She couldn't deny it anymore, or run from it like a coward. This human man was special to her in ways she could never explain. With a soul she could not clearly see, and a mind that matched her power. No matter how much she tried to ignore it, the truth would always prevail.

Cassandra took his head gently and rested it in her lap. Even though she was a gory dripping mess, and he was splattered with pieces of flesh and blood, she bent down and kissed his lips to hers. Taking her hand and gently caressing his face.

This was her human. And she must protect him. He could never learn the truth of what she had planned to do to him. What she had done to all the others. Things were different now. In a huge way.

But she still needed to return home with him. Maybe together they could find a way to help her people. Without killing all of the humans and turning full vampire. Perhaps there was another way.

Cassandra positioned him in her arms, and hovered her hand over his face. Instantly, he became clean, and all the blood and debris were removed from him. She did the same for herself, cleansing them of all the evidence from the terrible encounter. He didn't need to see the proof of how gruesome she could become. She didn't want him to see her as a monster.

She couldn't teleport with him, which would have been so much easier right about now. But instead, she carried him out to the car they drove up in. Outside, the normal sounds of the night had resumed. Crickets and animal calls echoed throughout the woods. Sounds she didn't hear before. It was her gifts that had canceled everything else out, so she could hear the danger. It was her body's way of protecting itself. But she had not listened to it. A fatal mistake she would never make again.

She carried Drago to the car and placed him inside on the passenger seat. She got in behind the wheel and closed the door. Just as she started the car, she remembered one last thing. The strange black box Drago always carried with him. It seemed important to him. She couldn't leave it behind. Teleporting back into the room, she saw the box on the floor to the side. She picked it up and looked at it. Wondering if she should look inside and see what he always kept hidden.

But the box was locked. She wondered curiously, if the key was that weird pendant he always wore on his neck.

Shrugging her shoulders, Cassandra teleported back inside the car, and put the vehicle in drive. She had watched the way they came to the boarding house, and remembered the path back to the plane. As she drove, her thoughts wandered to the one thing that seemed to be nagging her in the back of her head.

How had the same men from back in the US find them in France so quickly? And how was it they had known where they would be going, as if they'd been waiting for them?

Chapter Eighteen

Drago opened his eyes slowly and realized immediately that he was back on the plane. He was strapped into one of the seats in the back, with the chair pulled down so he could lay flat. There was an IV stuck in his arm giving him liquids, and his chest, although healed, had a faint scar across it. Driving his memory back to why it was there.

He unstrapped himself from the chair and sat up, his head clearing up after a few dizzying moments. Looking around in confusion, he didn't see anyone else in the plane. But he knew it wasn't flying itself.

Taking out the IV, Drago turned in the seat about to get up and search the aircraft.

"I wouldn't be so eager to get up right now, son. You'd lost a lot of blood."

Drago turned at the sound of Philip's voice. He came from the cockpit, and closed the door behind him.

"Philip what's going on? How did I get back here? Where's Cassandra?" Drago rushed out the words even as he stood up anyway. He wasn't some weakling. He wanted answers now.

Philip sighed and walked over to him, he sat in the seat across from him and gestured for Drago to sit back down. Waiting patiently for him.

Grunting in annoyance Drago sat down, not wanting to admit his head was still a bit fuzzy. He just wanted to know what the hell happened. And where was Cassandra?

"Who's flying the plane, Philip? Are you going to start talking or what?"

"Maybe if you'd shut the fuck up, I can." Philip answered so smoothly, that Drago remained silent. For the moment. He stared at him, waiting.

Philip sighed heavily and dragged his hand over his bald head. He looked up at Drago and shook his head at him.

"Your girlfriend is resting, so you can stop worrying, ok? She's in the further back compartment, cause she didn't want you to wake and see her as yet. She asked that you let her come to you on her own, when she gets up. It's still two hours to sunset so that won't be long. The plane is currently on auto-pilot."

Philip paused knowing Drago would have a lot more questions. Which he fired out right away.

"Wait a second, hold on. Two hours to sunset? How is that possible? It was after ten pm when we landed in Paris. And we were scheduled to meet you at eleven. The trip to Poland from there is only an hour. It should still be nightfall right now. How is it currently sunset?"

Drago's voice was rising in his agitation and confusion, and he looked at Philip as the realization began to hit him.

"Philip, give it to me straight, how long was I out?" He asked the question not really wanting to know the answer.

Philip stared at him a moment, not blinking an eye. Then said it without hesitation.

"You've been out for three days, Drago. A lot has happened since you went to the cottage in Paris."

Drago felt the wind rush out of him, as he heard the truth. Three days? What the hell happened to him?

Philip went on as if he had asked the question out loud.

"Your lady friend had returned with you within the hour as instructed. But you were out cold. It looked as if you were in a coma of sort, and nothing we did could wake you. You had lost too much blood, and was near death."

Philip paused as his face balled up in a brief mask of fury, just before he controlled it. He continued in his explanation.

"I knew she'd had something to do with it. The guilt was written all over her pretty face. But we both knew we couldn't take you to a hospital. She'd told me what happened to you guys. How you were ambushed at the cottage and almost killed."

Philip's face bore the look of a man riddled with guilt of his own. Was it because he'd told them it was safe, and it turned out it wasn't? Or was it something else?

"We had no choice but to keep you hidden here on the plane. And care for you until you woke up. Knowing you have people out there looking for you. But I couldn't just stay in Paris. My time was up. So I kept running my routes. Allowing you and

Cassandra to just ride along with me, until you recovered. During that time, I learned just what...and who she really is."

Philip paused and rubbed his hand over his mouth. As he chose his next words carefully. He had seen a lot of things within his day. But the bloody aftermath of what he'd seen in the cottage, after Cassandra told him what happened to Drago, was more than he had bargained for.

He hadn't believed her story at first. That they were ambushed, and she believed Adele had set them up. Turned out it was all true. When Philip investigated further, he discovered Adele had been approached by some strange men before they'd arrived. And offered a large sum of money to keep Drago and Cassandra within the house. Until they could apprehend them. But apparently the order had been shoot to kill for Drago. And take Cassandra alive. Paralyzing her with a special weapon they had contrived. But Cassandra explained how Drago had saved her life...again. Almost giving his up completely. His blood was enough to give her the strength to push out the poison, and regain her full power.

She had killed everyone on sight. Even Adele. The woman's body was found beheaded on the roof of her cottage. Her chest ripped open and her heart laying a few feet from her carcass.

Philip explained all of this to Drago in detail, going over every sordid part of the tale.

"You have no idea just what you're dealing with here, Drago." Philip said now, with a slight fear in his eyes.

"She didn't want to go to her home without you. So I've been making my runs, until you woke. Agreeing to head back to Poland the moment you recovered. What else could I say to her? I damn well wasn't going to say no! You didn't see what I saw back there. Drago, that woman is not human. I don't know what she is, but you need to get as far away from her as possible. Before she does to you what she did to those men back there. She almost killed you too!"

Drago sat quietly as he listened to everything Philip told him. The reality of it all hitting him like a ton of bricks.

It took him a moment to process it all, and put everything together.

So apparently, they had been followed. Adele, Philip's contact had set them up. But how had they known they would be there? Was it because of Philip? Drago could see that his old friend was genuinely pissed and worried for him. So it was obvious he hadn't betrayed them. But they'd known, nonetheless. They seemed to know their every move. How was that possible?

Then Drago's thoughts wandered to the woman he'd been willing to give his life for. The woman who in turn had saved his. She had killed them all. Just as he'd thought it was the end, that he would be meeting his maker, she had intervened and annihilated the entire threat. If what Philip said was true, she had used his blood to fight off the poison they had shot her with. And had almost taken all. But she didn't. And as far as Drago was concerned, if she'd needed it all, he would have gladly given it.

He looked up at Philip as he sat watching him. The expression on his face already telling him that he knew Drago would never walk away from Cassandra. It was pointless to even try to convince him further.

Philip shrugged and shook his head in resignation.

"Hey, I tried. It's your funeral, son." Philip said curtly.

Drago ignored the remark and looked towards the back of the plane.

"You said she's back there? Still asleep?"

Philip rolled his eyes impatiently as he knew that was the only thing on his mind. He didn't care about anything else at the moment.

"Yeah, behind those doors. You'll find her."

Drago got up from his seat without another word and headed to the back. It wasn't something he could explain to Philip. Or to anyone. He was connected to that woman in a way that defied reality. And he would not let anything, or anyone separate them.

He walked to the back and opened the door. Closing it behind him quickly. The area was pitch dark, and had most of the boxes from Philip's cargo runs piled up. But he could still see her. She was laying on a mat in the back, sprawled out on her side, and so still. A lifeless form so vulnerable, yet deadly.

Drago's heart lurched at the sight of her. There was so much he wanted to say and do. She had saved his life this time. And now, he wanted to celebrate that life with her. And remind himself that she was real.

He laid down beside her, and wrapped her body within his arms. Sheltering her cold flesh within his heat. She would feel him when she awakened, as it should be. She should feel the warmth and love of the man that would give his life for hers.

Chapter Nineteen

Cassandra opened her eyes and immediately knew he was there. It was like waking up into what the sun must be like to humans. Bright and beautiful all around. She was filled with a feeling of protection and security as she'd never known. And she didn't want it to end. But time waited for no one. And they had lost three days already. Days that they could not afford to lose.

Whatever Catalina had been trying to tell her, was somehow happening to other Carpathian women as well. The hunger cries were getting louder. More desperate. And Cassandra could feel the pain of her people even as she'd slumbered.

Turning in his arms, she looked up at his face, as he slept. Marveling at the fact that she still had him with her. It seemed as if he kept placing his life on the line for her, which meant he probably would again. But how could she willingly allow him to go through with it?

Cassandra sat up and gently touched him to nudge him awake. It was time she told him the truth, before they reached their destination. He had to know what was in store for him.

Drago woke up and smiled when he saw her face. Reaching for her hair as his muscular arms embraced her to him. Cassandra allowed herself to get lost in his kiss, if only for a moment. She would tell him. She just wanted to enjoy this pleasure right now.

He traced her face, as his lips caressed and massaged her with warm kisses. Opening her mouth so that he could feel the delicious texture of her tongue on his. He held her close as they lay together on the floor, breathing in her essence and molding the shape and curve of her body to his hardened form.

"Drago..." Cassandra sighed into his lips, as he pulled off her jeans. Relieving himself of his own.

"Shhh.... just feel. I need you to just feel me."

Drago whispered the words to her, as he spread her thighs, and entered into her smooth and wet heat of desire.

His sank deep, burying himself into her cocoon, and gripping onto her round buttocks so that he could thrust deeper. Filling her ever so slowly, drawing out the sweet torture of the most pleasurable sensation he'd ever known.

Drago looked into her eyes as he began to move within her, speaking to her in a way that only their souls would understand. Needing her to see without eyes, and feel without touch.

"This is all that matters..." Drago breathed into her lips as he pumped his devotion within her body and soul. "Nothing else. Just this. Just me and you...and what we have right now..."

He lifted her legs higher and delved into her with increased vigor now. Stroking long and firm with every thrust, as he began to pound her body like a man crazed and insane.

Cassandra cried out in ecstasy, throwing her head back and arching perfectly, as she took him with every thrust and stroke. Matching his rhythm pound for pound, and opening her mind to him. But this time, she felt his mind open as well. And it was like an avalanche of eruption and power.

Drago shouted out in pleasure, as he felt her soul touch his, a union that was cataclysmic, and explosive. He held onto her body as their skin began to heat up and glow with fiery like embers and small flames licking at them. But they were both oblivious to this, dancing together as their bodies intertwined within a vortex of passion.

Cassandra felt the ball of heat rising within her loins, lifting to join together in unison with his. And they hit their peak together, shattering light and colors within their mind, that caused them both to throw their heads back in the beauty of their connection. The aftershock and tremors of the violently passionate encounter was without equal. It took them a while to recover, satisfied to simply lay within each other's arms while their souls gloried in the newfound bond.

It was Drago that said it first. The words coming out before either of them could stop it.

"I love you."

Cassandra's breath hitched within her throat, and her eyes turned from green to chocolate brown. Something within her trembled and moved. And that's when she realized it for the first time. The shock almost paralyzed her.

She could see his soul. And it was filled with lights of all kinds. There was darkness in there as well, but it was not compared to the beautiful blinding colors that lit her mind. It was the most precious thing she'd ever seen. Looking into his eyes, she saw him for the first time. A human man that was good and bad. But his good outweighed his darkness. He had done terrible things. Yes, but he'd also done good things. And the scale tipped, as she judged him to be worthy of the Carpathian blood. A man that was strong enough to endure their essence and procreate the life of their species.

Cassandra lay there on the ground, so shocked, that she didn't recognize the sound before it was too late. The scream that rose from Philip was so gruesome, it felt as the windows shook and trembled with it.

Drago's eyes widened in terror, as he stared at her. Leaping off of her to pull on his pants.

"That was Philip! Something's wrong!"

Drago shouted out as he flung open the cargo door to race out and help his friend.

"Drago no! Don't go out there!"

But Cassandra was too late. Drago had run headfirst into the plane, and encountered what she'd been hoping to avoid.

The Carpathian people. It was several of the women. The judges. All standing there in the plane, in their sheer white dresses. Philip's blood was all over them, and his body lay in tatters across the cockpit.

"Philip!" Drago charged at the women, using his knives and taking down two of them. They leaped at him, crawling onto the ceiling and surrounding him.

"No! Don't kill him!" Cassandra raced across the plane to stop the women, using her powers to leap at them and slashed the head of one of the women.

The moment she did that, the remaining Carpathians all turned to her as one, their eyes glowing red with rage.

"Traitor." They said in unison.

Three of them grabbed her arms and slashed several parts of her body, so that she would bleed out slowly. It wouldn't kill her, just make her weak and powerless.

One of the women, a tall one with silver hair, dodged one of Drago's knives, and caught it in the air. Throwing it back at him to land in his arm.

Drago cried out in pain, as he fell to his knees.

"You bitch!" He cursed at her, as she came at him to sever his head.

"No! He's the one. We need him. We can't kill him like the others. His blood is useful to us."

Cassandra shouted out as she knelt on the ground, drained and tired from blood loss.

The Carpathian stopped just short of castrating him, and looked at him with red glowing eyes.

"Is he now? We shall see. After all, we may not need him anymore, Cassandra. Even though you clearly botched this mission. You still brought us a man. And if his blood is pure, all the better."

The one that stood in front of Drago spoke in a dark and menacing tone. She smiled devilishly at him, as the news hit like a ton of bricks.

He looked accusingly at Cassandra, the confusion and hurt was plain in his eyes, as he knelt on the floor holding his arm with the knife still in it. But his pain was coming more from his heart.

"What do you mean, can't kill him like the others, Cassandra? You told me you let the others go. That if they couldn't help, you set them free."

The Carpathian woman standing before him laughed wickedly, and answered before Cassandra could.

"Is that what she told you? Oh you foolish human man. You creatures are so pathetic. We should've killed you all long ago. That is what we do. We find, we judge, and we kill. You are here to serve as food. Nothing more. Your blood will fill our bellies with replenishment as was intended of your kind."

"Stop lying Patrona! We only kill when necessary. Our mission is to find help. We only kill the dark ones. Not the innocent." Cassandra spoke up in anger as she panted in exasperation.

"Oh you see, you were gone too long this time, Cassandra. Things have changed a bit. A new order has been set in place. We no longer are going to sit around for centuries waiting for a human male that is pure in soul to save us. It has been decided. All humans are now forfeit. And the judgement has been given. They will all die. Starting with your human pet here, as one of the first."

"No!" Cassandra shouted in disbelief as they grabbed Drago roughly off his feet.

But her shock at this horrible news was nothing compared to the pain of betrayal she saw on Drago's face, when he looked at her.

"Philip was right all along. You're nothing but a monster."

Drago said the chilling words as he was carted away. His eyes damning her to a hell worse than the pit. Philip had landed right where they'd asked him to. In the Carpathian Mountains, near a spot by the Morskie Lake, in Poland. It was Cassandra's guess that he hadn't told them because he'd wanted to give them a bit of privacy, knowing they were in the back making love. But it was the last bit of kindness Drago's friend would ever do for him. As he'd unknowingly landed right as the Carpathian women had emerged from their underground lair. To exact a vengeance on man that had been centuries in the making.

That was the warning Catalina had been trying to send her. But she couldn't hear it, because she'd been too connected to Drago.

Cassandra was left behind on the plane, still on her knees. The pain and enormity of what was now happening, was closing in on her. And she was too weak to do anything about it.

But she couldn't let them kill Drago. She had to do something. She had to find a way to get through to the women before they turned full vampire.

Chapter Twenty

The camp they had secured deep within the Carpathian Mountains was assured to be the most secure place they could assess and gather intel. So far, his guy had been correct. They could see everything, and remain undetected, even from the dreaded Carpathians.

Edward used his binoculars to watch as the plane landed. They'd been waiting for them for the past two days. Knowing their arrival would bring out the Carpathians, and reveal to them their secret resting grounds.

He and his people had known ever since the showdown in Paris France, where Drago and Cassandra were headed and why. The plan had worked marvelously, and he was surprised Drago had never caught on.

Edward focused his binoculars and smirked, watching as seven beautiful and ethereal looking women, emerged from beneath the ground and headed for the plane. He silently stood and observed the massacre of Philip Crouch, through the windows of the aircraft. Watching as the blood splattered the glass. And then coolly took note as they apprehended Drago and took him prisoner. Leaving a wounded Cassandra behind to fend for herself.

The cold smile spread on his hardened face, as he followed the women's progress. Taking Drago below with them into their underground lair.

Edward lowered his binoculars and turned back towards one of his men, who had been taking silent photographs of everything, with a specially designed camera.

"Did you get all of that, Pearson? The murder, the abduction, everything?" Edward asked him stoically.

"I got it, sir." Pearson answered quietly. His facial expression said it all.

Edward nodded briefly, and looked over at the armed forces he'd brought along with him. Highly skilled men that were trained for a special kind of combat. Ones that dealt with things not of this world. Their weapons were designed to target the threat and attack its weakness. In this case, a blinding light created to emit the same powerful rays of the sun. He knew the weapon worked expertly. Already having used it on one of the unsuspecting creatures who was caught wandering around the lake when they'd first arrived.

Edward smiled in satisfaction, remembering how the tall and slim female with long black hair had screamed in terror and pain, as he'd first severed her hand from her body, then watched as her ashes were blown away in the wind. He had made certain to leave the immediate area before any others arrived. They hadn't known the hiding place at the time, so it had been wiser to wait for Drago and Cassandra to arrive, and have it revealed to them.

Edward walked towards his main tent within the small base camp, and prepared to ready his men for the invasion.

It had almost been too easy. The way they were able to find them. All thanks to the incompetence of Drago Brown.

Edward chuckled and shook his head, thinking about how foolish the man was, following a creature to her home territory. Believing her evil lies. He had known Drago was a weak one, and that was how they'd found him.

The battle in Paris, had just been a decoy. A distraction. Something to keep them away long enough so that the tracker could be placed within Philip's plane. The tracker enabled them to hear everything that was said and done. And it was easy to replace Philip's delivery man with one of their own guys. When Philip met with the guy in Paris to deliver the assigned weapons cargo, he had no idea it was one of Edward's own men who had entered his plane and secretly planted the tracker directly in the cockpit. It was designed to pick up destinations, and any voice recognition within several feet of the plane. They were able to hear everything. Even the pathetic interaction between Drago and the creature.

Edward was repulsed and felt Drago got exactly what he deserved. A man like him should've known better than to sleep with the enemy.

But none of that mattered now. It was finally time to bring the final remains of these creatures to destruction. Something his very ancestors had started so long ago. Many had thought he was crazy, and his own family had never believed in the legends that were handed down through his history line. A legend of the vampire. A very real and dangerous threat to society. Not a myth, as the creatures wanted the humans to believe. But very real.

Edward Beckman Jr. came from a very long line of hunters. Men that belonged to a secret organization that the general public would never know about. The very men who were now fighting by his side, were also avid members. This was something the government didn't even know about. He was careful to give a good reason for the use of firearms, but never explained what the weapons could do.

For years, Edward had covered up his secret mission to find the Carpathian people, by creating a camouflage case. Making the government believe he was looking for people with special abilities, like telepathy and psychic phenomena. They would have laughed him out of a career had he revealed he was searching for vampires.

But he was very convincing. And for a while, the government had funded his operation. He'd never had any real leads until Cassandra Martin showed up on the map.

A series of random and inconsistent disappearances all across the world, would never gain notice for any particular country, unless someone knew exactly what to look for. And that someone had been Edward. Nearing retirement, he was almost out of options, and had exhausted all leads, until he'd had a break in the case five years ago. A lead that was certain to guide him directly to Cassandra. But it had all gone to hell. And his whole operation had caved in. The government ceasing all activities, and demanding the closing of the mission.

Even though Edward had to close up shop, he had simply bided his time. Growing more men within the secret organization who believed in his cause. And now, because of his patience, that day had finally come. He knew where the underground hideout was located, and there was no escape for the Carpathians this time. This time, he would finish what his ancestors had started.

Edward placed several guns loaded with the special rays onto his weapons belt. And then hooked a rifle around his shoulder. He and his men were ready. Once he gave the word, they would close in on the lair, blocking the entrance, and surrounding all exit points. There was no getting away this time. The Carpathians would finally meet their end.

Chapter Twenty One

Cassandra slowly made her way out of the plane, and headed towards the underground lair. Every step was excruciating for her, and she needed blood desperately. But she couldn't stop. She had to find a way to convince the order to stop the judges from executing him. To turn their minds back to their legacy and purpose.

This was all her fault, Cassandra thought to herself as she found the entrance to her home. She was too weak to teleport, so she would have to make the journey the hard way.

Panting heavily, Cassandra lowered herself through the narrow passageway and used what was left of her strength to cover it back up. The tunnel that was usually so easy to navigate was now a burden. As each downward slip, caused more blood to seep out of her. Grunting in pain, she bore down on the blinding agony, and used her legs to slide down through the opening. To a human, the caves would be buried too far down for them to breathe naturally, without the assistance of the Carpathians.

Cassandra finally made it through the wide mouth of the entry point, and cried out in pain as she fell headfirst through it. Hurtling with a hard impact as she hit the ground. Her wounds opened up further, and her blood pooled onto the floor.

For a moment, she considered just laying there, and letting herself bleed out. It would be a slow death, but it was no less than what she deserved.

And that was when she saw it. Dust particles. Ashes from one of the Carpathians. Cassandra sat up and frowned. Her people would never kill one of their own like this. This was not their way.

Moving closer to the pile of dust, she saw that it had come from the mouth of the cave. The entry point above ground had a trail of glittering substance that lined it. Showing where the ashes had fallen through. It was the Carpathian custom, that when one died abnormally, their ashes would find the home of their resting place. But this was only possible if the Carpathian died within a few feet from the grounds. If it was anyplace else, the essence would simply wither away.

Cassandra slowly crawled closer to the pile of glittering dust, and very carefully reached her hand towards it, to touch the soft and powdery ashes.

The moment she did, her body jerked in reaction, stiffening with the pain of death of one of her own. She could see them clearly in her mind's eye. The flashes of light pouring through her like sharp daggers.

Cassandra cried out in agony, as she saw more than she was ready for. As it was finally revealed to her what happened.

Catalina. Her dear and sweet spirit sister who had emerged from the safety of the caves for her, had been brutally killed by the humans. They had a special device, they were using. She could see it all as if it was happening to her, in her mind's eye.

They had surprised Catalina at the lake, as she was still gathering the water elements needed for the potion Cassandra had instructed her to make. The water from the lake had healing ingredients within it. A substance that would either feed them, or kill them all. Cassandra had told Catalina to go to the water, if anything ever happened to her, and she didn't return. She'd told her to mix the water with their blood, and that it should replace their endless need for sustenance. It was a risk. One that could very well kill all remaining Carpathian women. But if anything happened to Cassandra while out hunting, her people needed a plan for survival. She had instructed her sister to do it only if there were no other options left.

Cassandra felt the pain begin from the pit of her loins, and slowly rise to the heart of her, flaming up to her blood red eyes. The rage was instant.

She craned back her head and screamed in fury. Her body shaking from the effects of reliving what her spirit sister had endured. She had called for her. Tried to reach her. But their communication had been blocked because of Drago. Because of the human man that she now knew could save them all.

Cassandra collapsed on the ground in helpless tears. Tears she didn't even realize she could produce, ever since she came into contact with Drago. It all came back to him.

It wasn't his fault Catalina was dead. It was her own. She'd been too stubborn to see the signs. Had been so used to hunting men with dark souls, she had given up looking for anything else. From the moment she met him, her powers had connected with him. And that is why she could not see his soul until he'd chosen to open it up. She could not teleport with him, unless he touched his mind with hers. They could not save her people, until they both finally admitted who they were to each other.

And now, there was another threat in addition to the Carpathian women turning full vampire. The humans knew their location. And they had in their possession a device that could destroy them all. Cassandra believed they were even now somewhere close. She didn't have much time left.

Picking herself up, she knelt on the ground before her sister's ashes. A pile of forgotten dust no one had even noticed. She closed her eyes and placed her hands within the glittering particles. Speaking softly into the atmosphere.

May your life, be my life. May your pain be my pain. Allow your essence to live within my spirit. And my strength to keep your light alive. I am one with my spirit sister."

Cassandra recited the blood ritual of the spiritual sisterhood bond. And slowly, the ashes began to rise up. They surrounded her, and sifted into her wounds, sealing them up. Burying deep into her flesh until the dust vanished and became a part of her skin.

Cassandra gasped, raising her head as power slammed within her body. A rejuvenation of the soul, as she felt the essence of her sister within her mind. A connection that will now never be severed again.

Filled with new vigor and strength, Cassandra stood up within the caves and began to race towards the gate. She knew that was where they had taken Drago. The place where all human men came to die.

***

Drago grunted as he was thrown into a large open space, a small circle of flames immediately erupted around him and kept him trapped within the area.

He held onto his still bleeding arm, although the knife had been removed, as he stood up. Watching the six women that gathered around him. Just standing and staring at him, like he was an animal in a circus. Drago scowled back at them, standing with his feet braced apart, ready for anything. He didn't care what powers they possessed; they weren't going to take him down again.

Drago remained quiet, not saying a word. He wasn't going to give these creatures any ammunition to use against him.

Finally, one of them spoke up. She was beautiful as all the others, slim and with yellow blond hair and cold red and yellow eyes. She wore a long clingy and silky white dress, identical to all the rest of the women, that looked more like a night gown. She smiled slowly, and tilted her head as if observing a child.

"Look my sisters, he still has so much fight left in him. Isn't that so cute? How he thinks he still has a chance?" The female laughed and was joined together with her sisters.

Drago refused to be baited. He remained silent.

Once they saw they could get no reaction from him, they gave up the banter.

"Cassandra believed that you are somehow special to us, but I do not see it. Your humanity stinks. And your blood reeks of impurities. You are no different from the rest of them, and we shall prove it this night. There is no need to perform our usual tests. You have been judged, and found guilty of your dark soul. You and all your human people will die. And your death will be the beginning of our reign."

Drago spit into the fire, and smirked at the woman as she finished her speech.

"Fuck you."

He uttered the words with a straight face. She and all her evil creatures could go straight to hell. None of it mattered anymore to him.

Suddenly the floor opened up, and he fell swiftly through the ground. The temperature getting hotter the further down he went.

Drago tried to keep his balance upright, but it was moving too fast, he fell hard, as he encountered the ground once again and rolled, almost knocking him into a new circle of flames. He used his good arm to slow down his spiral, and he scraped his flesh to a sudden halt, as the motion finally stopped.

Drago panted heavily for a moment before getting to his feet. He looked around, the circle of flames lowering until they disappeared completely. Now it was absolutely dark. The heat almost unbearable, and the loss of sight would cause a weaker man to go crazy. But Drago kept his head.

Remaining in place and not moving. He didn't know where he was, or who was with him. It was best to be still till he was sure.

Suddenly, a flaming torch came to life along the wall, and there was enough light for him to see around him.

Drago began to wish the darkness would return.

There were bodies everywhere. Piles and piles of carcasses, and bones, and decaying flesh. Some were old, and others were as fresh as if they'd been thrown in only a week ago. All were men. Dead and mutilated human men.

Drago felt the bile rising in his throat, as the stench and heat of the cooking flesh overtook his senses. Some of the men looked really young. Like teenage boys. Young men that hadn't even lived yet. This is what they called judgement? This was an annihilation.

Drago fell to his knees coughing and choking, trying to control his need to vomit. He focused his mind and bore down on his emotions. Blocking out the attack on his senses. He used the same skills that had kept him alive during his time in the prison camps.

Just as he'd felt his composure was back in place, Drago's eyes fell upon the rotting skeleton of a nearby corpse. His bones were almost turning to dust, but some of his tattered clothes still clung to his body. But it's what was draped around the skeleton's neck, that caused Drago to get up and walk over to the bones. His steps were slow and measured, as his heart began to pound. He stopped in front of it, and bent down before the rotting shell.

Around the neck of the skull, was a silver chain. Drago lifted the chain and looked at it. It was attached to a small pendant, a silver ball, like a clear pearl with slight colors sifting through it. There was none like it other than the one he had. The only gift from their father at the age of five and eight, after which they'd never seen him again. Drago always kept his around his neck. The only time he didn't have it was when he was incarcerated. And it was secured within the black box. His brother had the other one. His brother Darren, whom he'd been looking for over the past five years. A victim of these creatures, who had taken him and many other men for far longer than he'd ever believed.

Drago was silent as he looked at his brother's remains. He touched the skeleton, as his emotions went cold and hollow inside. Now he understood why he was here. How could he have forgotten his main purpose?

Drago looked at his brother's corpse and stood up, staring up into the mouth of the pit. It was time for the Carpathians to receive a judgement of their own.

Chapter Twenty Two

Cassandra raced over to the entrance of the gate, the wide opening deep within the caves they kept sectioned off for the humans. She raised her hand, and a thin electrical blue light began to spread from it. She lifted it against the shield, and felt resistance.

"What the hell is this?" Cassandra muttered in confusion. The judges dared to try and prevent a gates keeper from entering into the gate? They were fools if they thought they could stop her!

Cassandra closed her eyes and increased in power, her entire body lighting up within blue flames and lighting. She flung a ball of power at the shield around the gate, and it trembled with the force of it. Creating a spiderweb crack all over the surface. She took her fist and punched through the crack, shattering the force field altogether.

Cassandra didn't waste a moment as she raced over to the center, where the judges still stood around, waiting for her.

"What the hell are you all doing? This is my human, I chose him! Now I demand that you release him."

Cassandra walked directly up to the other women, and stared them down. Her clothes had changed into the customary white dress of the Carpathians, and her black curls were in a disarray around her face. She was a vision of fury and passion. They knew she was more powerful than they were. But it was not the judges who answered her.

"Cassandra, stand down. This was our decision. They are following orders."

Cassandra turned around to face the other six women within the order. The elders who were charged in keeping their women safe. She looked at them in confusion.

"Why would you all do this? What's happened to you? This is not our way!"

Cassandra pleaded with the leader and head of the order, Mariella. As she stood regally among the women.

Mariella, her lovely smooth brown skin glowing and her lavender and blue eyes sparkling, watched

Cassandra with a resignation and heaviness. She shook her head as she sighed.

"We had no choice, Cassandra. Our people are starving. And the humans cannot save us. We have tried the queen's way for centuries. With no success. It is time to take our place above ground, and control the human menace."

"If you do that, you violate more than just our legacy. Have you all forgotten what we will become?" Cassandra shot back at her in anger.

"You all have forgotten about the legends, the tales. Of the empties and what they did to our people. How they divided us, and eventually caused us to have war with the humans. We lost our men because of it."

"No, Cassandra. We lost our men because of the humans." The one called Simone spoke, she was a member of the order. "They hunted them, remember? And they will do the same for us if given the chance."

The other women murmured in agreement at this, and Cassandra saw in their eyes they wouldn't listen. The humans were about converge on them, and they would in turn wage war on the humans.

There would be no end to it. Unless she could show them proof.

"Let me go down to him. I'll show you that he can change things. He's not like the others. The queen was right. We can use him to help us procreate and grow. I know we can. Just let me prove it to you. Please."

Cassandra pleaded with Mariella, knowing she was the only one who may see reason. All she needed was to talk to Drago.

Mariella sighed, looking at Cassandra with pity. She nodded her head.

"Alright, I'll allow it. But only for a few minutes, Cassandra. If this human cannot show us anything, then we will kill him. If he tries to hurt you, we will kill him. Do you understand?"

Cassandra nodded her head briskly and stepped into the small circle of flames. She teleported herself instantly down into the pit below. Where the heat was excruciating. Any normal human would be dead by now, their flesh melting away. But not Drago Brown.

He stood off in the corner of the large pit, looking down at a skeleton and holding onto a chain.

She approached him cautiously, not really knowing what to expect.

"Drago....it's me, Cassandra. We need to talk."

She didn't receive a response from him. He simply kept his back to her, while staring down at the chain.

Cassandra took a deep breath and continued to talk.

"I know I lied to you, Drago. I lied about what could happen if you weren't able to help us. I did some bad things, really bad things, and I'm sorry for it now. I forgot my purpose, my mission. I got lost in my bitterness. My obsession to save my people. I was filled with an emptiness, as if I already was one of the empties. And then I met you. And you changed everything."

"I never told you my real reason for deciding to come along and help you. Did you ever wonder about that?" Drago interrupted her smoothly. He placed the chain in his pocket, and turned around to face her.

Something within Cassandra shrank back when she saw the cold and shattered look in his eyes. There was nothing there. She could no longer see his soul.

"I agreed because you mentioned the name, Carpathian. A name which had landed me in jail four years ago."

Drago smirked coldly, and stared at her with lifeless eyes.

"You see Cassandra, I had just recently been discharged from the military. Honors and everything. I was going to make a fresh start for me and my younger brother. He'd been in a lot of trouble since I'd been gone, and I was hoping that me being there would bring him back to himself."

Drago felt the bitterness and pain grip his heart as he thought of his brother. A life that had been taken and wasted away.

"But I was too late. When I got home, he was gone. Vanished. No one could find any trace of him. Police wouldn't help me, government officials, no one. He was just another missing case that fell through the cracks."

Cassandra felt her blood begin to race, as she started to put the pieces together, one by one. The chain he'd placed in his pocket. The skeleton shell he'd been standing over, watching with cold and vacant eyes.

She took a step back, shaking her head slowly in disbelief as it was starting to hit her.

Drago continued on, watching her retreat with damning eyes.

"And then I was approached by these strange men in suits. They told me they knew what happened to my brother, and that they could help me find him. I was recruited into an organization that no one else knows about. They trained me, gave me more skills than I ever learned in the military. Then they sent me in search of the one they were looking for. They didn't have a face yet or clear description. Just leads. And a weird sounding name. Carpathians."

Drago paused as Cassandra's eyes widened in shock, enjoying the slight fear he saw cross her lovely face.

"I got nothing but dead ends, and was told if I was ever caught, they would claim to not know me. I could never reveal I was with them, and would get no help from them. But they promised me they could help me find my brother. And since they were the only ones who'd offered, I took the deal." Drago shrugged his shoulders and watched her, wanting her to know it all.

"So I went along with everything. Going on these ridiculous missions they sent me, and always carrying the black box they gave me."

Cassandra's eyes widened further at finding out about the mysterious black box.

"Yes, it belonged to the agency. I was to keep it with me at all times so they could track me anywhere I was. But one day, I went on an assigned mission with three untrained men. They were sloppy. Didn't follow orders. We were supposed to retrieve intel on a lead within the Russian government. But they killed everyone, and we had to leave the country quickly. When we entered back into the US the FBI and other officials were waiting for us. Our cover was blown. But instead of the fools just surrendering, they blew up two government buildings, and hundreds of people were killed in the chaos. I was caught and arrested. Labeled a Russian spy, under my fictious name, James Freeman, because I couldn't reveal my real contacts. All of my real identity had been wiped clean from the system. So once captured, I truly was on my own. They had abandoned me. Before I was taken, I had placed the black box within a safety chest. So they didn't even know if I was alive or not. Not that it would have mattered either way. That part of the government kept everything very classified. Never revealing my apprehension. So even the CIA wasn't aware of what happened to me. I was taken away and served with the death penalty. I was in that prison for four years. Luckily, I still had the skills they'd taught me. I was able to form anonymous contacts outside of the jail. With money I had stashed away. I planned my escape, and that was how you saw me on the news."

Drago paused and looked around at the pit, then his eyes rested again on his brother's bones.

"Ever since I got out, and obtained the black box again, I have been feeding them information. That's how they always knew where I was. I was allowing them to track us. All up until we were at the hotel in Waverly, and you didn't kill me. You could've drained my blood, but didn't. So when you mentioned going to the Carpathian Mountains, I turned the tracker off. I had wanted to see for myself if this was all real. And that's why they came after us. Tried to corner us at that gas station. They knew I was going against protocol. I was going against the organization. But apparently, they had a tracker I didn't know about. One they knew I'd never take off.

Drago touched his pendant, and she knew.

Chapter Twenty Three

Cassandra stood as he told her everything. How he was all connected to the men who had tried to kill her. Who wanted all of her people dead.

"So you'd been working with them? Leading them here to my home the whole time? It was all just a trap?" She asked him in a shaky voice.

Drago ignored the rush of emotion at the sound of her pain, and shoved it down within him. He smiled cruelly.

"You are the last one to cast any blame, sweetheart. Not after what you did. Like I said, I didn't know about the other tracker. I had destroyed the one inside the box. I discovered the small chip when I was looking at the one that belongs to my brother."

Drago's voice slightly hitched when he mentioned his brother, and Cassandra knew that if she possessed a heart, it would be in a million pieces right now.

"I noticed when looking at his that it didn't have a small circle at the bottom of it, like mine did. Something I didn't recognize till now. But the tracker in my pendant didn't explain how they were able to know where we were going before we even got there."

"It must have been the plane." Cassandra said quietly, her eyes filled with regret and pain.

"I told Philip everything about our destination, while you were knocked out. And how to land there. The exact location. They were listening because of a bug they planted on the plane."

"Are you implying that Philip was a traitor?"

Drago took a threatening step towards her, and Cassandra stepped back quickly holding up her hands. She looked up at the mouth of the pit, hoping the women didn't see it as an attempt on her life.

"No, Drago. I know Philip had nothing to do with it. He loved you. They must have slipped it on the plane somehow while we were in Paris."

Drago thought about it for a moment, and closed his eyes as it hit him. The attack at the house, had been a set up. It was all decoy. He should have known, since that was one of things Edward had taught him in the agency. How could he have missed it?

As he stood with his fists balled, battling the death of his friend and what happened to his brother, Cassandra took a chance and stepped towards him.

His eyes shot open and stared at her, they were like piercing daggers. She stopped dead, and tried to plead with him.

"Drago, it's obvious we both lied to each other. And I'm sorry. I'm sorry for what I was and what I did. Yes, I killed many men. Hunted them and judged their souls. All I saw was darkness and decay among the human race. We were told by our queen long ago, if we could not find one to save us, we should destroy them all. So now that is what my sisters all want to do. But you can help us, Drago. It doesn't have to be this way. War between humans and Carpathians can be stopped right now, if me and you join together."

Drago was consumed by his pain. He couldn't hear her, or see past it. It was too late for both of them. They had crossed a line that could never be undone.

He turned his back on her and looked at the dried up bones of his brother. His helpless and foolish brother. Not even he had deserved a fate like this. No human did.

"It's no use anymore, Cassandra. Whatever we may have had, is done. You have your duties, and I have mine. There's nothing more to be said about it. Get away from me."

Drago said the words as a warning, and Cassandra wept quietly, still taking a step towards him. He turned around and shouted into her face.

"I said get the fuck away from me, you bitch!"

Drago raised his hand as if to hit her, and he was instantly catapulted across the pit. He crashed into the pile of bones, landing in a crumpled heap.

"No! Don't hurt him!"

Cassandra created a force field around Drago just as the ball of flames would have turned him into dust.

She shouted up into the mouth of the pit. "I said leave him! I understand, and will do as you wish. Just please...leave him alone."

The tears fell from her eyes as she begged her sisters. The ball of flames disappeared. And she heard Mariella's calm voice in her mind.

"Come back up to us, Cassandra. There's nothing left for you down there. Just dead human bones. All worthless. Nothing more."

Cassandra wept in full force, keeping her back to Drago now. She couldn't bear to look at him again. He had become her entire world. Showed her what the light could be like. And now her world was dark once again.

She wiped her tears away and stood up. Her head lowered in acceptance. They were right. There was nothing more she could do. Her voice came out as a hollow whisper, as she spoke without turning around.

"Goodbye, Drago. I just wanted you to know.... I love you too."

She instantly disappeared, teleporting back up to the surface. All Drago had left of her, was a sweet smell of flowers that was uniquely her scent. It traveled to him within the pit of death, and wrapped around his empty soul.

Giving into his pain, Drago threw back his head and screamed in rage. He screamed, until his echoes filled the pit around him.

***

"The humans are coming!" One of the builders, who constantly kept watch over the caves, came running down the pathway of tunnels. Her long brown hair flew out behind her, and her pale face was stricken with fear.

The other Carpathian women began to chatter loudly in nervousness and uncertainty. The humans had never known of their location. And it was impossible to find. So how could they be there?

Cassandra filled in the women of the order as quickly as she could.

"They tracked the plane I used to come here. The man I thought could help was working for them. He's a spy. So they know where we are."

"I told you we should've killed him!" Simone shouted at her in anger.

"It won't make a difference Simone. They're here now. We need to take action." Cassandra said impatiently.

"They can never get through the wards we have surrounding the caves. We are safe." Mariella said calmly.

But Cassandra shook her head sadly. She had to tell them.

"They have a way in. They killed Catalina, and she carried with her the secrets to the passageway. Secrets I had given her." She paused as the emotion filled her chest. "They severed her hand and will use the symbol on her palm to enter."

Mariella turned now with outraged fury, grabbing Cassandra's shoulders roughly.

"Why would you do that? Not only did you break our sacred oath to never reveal the passageways, except only to the gate keepers. You put your own spirit sister in danger by sending her above ground? By herself?! You fool!" Mariela smacked Cassandra hard across the face.

Cassandra felt the sting as her face swung with the impact. It was no more than she deserved. The tears were renewed as they fell from her eyes. She hung her head in shame and guilt, as she wept.

Mariella frowned in confusion as she lifted Cassandra's face to her inspection. She searched her eyes, looking in them with wonder and disbelief.

"Are these tears falling from your eyes, Cassandra? Human tears?"

Cassandra was too emotional to understand what it all meant. The loud boom that suddenly rocked the caves interrupted the moment, and they were all brought back to the matter at hand.

"What are we going to do? We were never trained to fight the humans, only protect them!" Bruna shouted out in panic.

"But I was." Cassandra said quietly. The tears drying up, and were replaced by the red glow of the Carpathian hunger. The six women who were judges joined her, as they also had experience dealing with the human scum.

Cassandra resolved in her mind that she would fix what she had messed up. She would save her people. It was because of her actions they were all in danger now. And it was up to her to save them all.

"They have a device with them that can destroy us on contact." Cassandra instructed the women, as they readied for battle.

"We need to use our speed before they can access it. Cut off their heads and arms. Do not allow them to use their weapons. These are our caves; we know them better than the humans. Remain hidden until the last possible moment. We will attack when I give the signal, using our minds to communicate."

Cassandra looked at them all. Her sisters. This was never supposed to happen. But she would protect them all by any means necessary. Even if it meant her death.

They headed down the tunnels, as all the other Carpathian women hid deeper within the caves.

Chapter Twenty Four

Drago felt the ground rumble, and the walls around the pit begin to crack and shake. But none of that mattered to him. He remained on his knees next to his brother's bones, looking at the identical pendant he wore. The one that was free of the tracking chip.

Suddenly there was a slight noise behind him, like a scuffling sound. The place was getting hotter, and the dim lighting of the torch only cast shadows that spread the darkness and gave very little light. But even though he was resigned to his fate, it didn't mean he had to go without a fight.

Grabbing a bone from one of the other corpses, Drago stood up and swung out viciously, aiming a strike at whatever was coming at him. He narrowly missed the small and dainty pale faced woman, as she stood in wide eyed panic, her hands covering her face in fear.

"Please! Please don't hurt me! I'm just here to deliver a message to you."

The female was clearly terrified of him, and cowered like a rabbit caught by the wolf.

Drago had the urge to drive the bone directly into her chest, ending her miserable existence. It was such a strong feeling that he had to fight for the control he was so well known for. Getting a grip on his emotions, he slowly lowered the bone and looked at the woman with distaste.

"Why are you here?" He asked her in a biting tone. His face was a mask of venom.

The Carpathian woman hesitated at first, looking as if she was thinking of running away instead of talking. But she swallowed, and took a deep breath, looking up at him. Drago saw that she had silver eyes and bright blue hair.

"I have a message for you, from Cassandra. She asked me to give this to you with only one word."

The woman shakily handed him a small blue crystal shaped in the form of a star. She dropped it into his hand careful not to touch him. And then looked up at him with panic in her eyes.

"Run."

Drago watched as she vanished right before him. The chilling word leaving an echo in the heated air that was almost close to suffocating him.

He looked down at the crystal star in his palm. The sweat was now pouring off of his skin, as he fell to his knees. The air in the pit was almost gone. If he was going to get out of there alive, he needed to do it now.

Breathing heavily, he turned the crystal over in his hand, not sure what he was supposed to do with it. Cassandra said use it to run. But how?

Then suddenly he remembered how Cassandra had used her gifts to attack the men following them back in Virginia. She had used a pulsing light from her hands and body.

His vision was getting blurry, as the heat in the pit now became flames. They were licking along the walls, and headed towards him. Fighting to focus, Drago looked at his brother's bones, and glanced at the chain he held in his hand again. He would have something to take back that he could bury for his brother. He placed it around his neck and staggered to his feet.

"Here goes nothing."

Drago took the crystal and pressed it into his hand. Amazingly, the crystal began to bury itself into his palm, disappearing into his skin and caused his hand to glow with blue electrical flames.

Panting, he lifted his hand up facing the oncoming fire, and it immediately made a pathway for him. The flames parted and revealed a passageway out of the pit. One that was swiftly closing.

Drago charged through it, leaping headfirst into the opening, as it closed shut the moment he went through.

For a few precious seconds, he took deep heaving breaths of the cooling air outside the pit. Steadying his heart, and regaining his composure. As he stood up, he vaguely realized that his shoulder was also healed. The flesh wound completely gone as if it had never been there.

He lifted his palm and saw that the crystal had formed a tattoo on the inside of his hand. It was the shape of the star, and outlined in blue.

Drago thought of Cassandra, and felt the walls of the tunnels shake even stronger now. She had saved him again, even though he had turned from her. She'd given him the way out.

Not wasting another moment, Drago held up his palm and used the embedded crystal to make a pathway out of the tunnels. Running at breakneck speed to avoid the collapse of the caves.

He emerged on the other side, crawling his way out of the cliffs, and coming out on the far north side of the mountain.

Drago fell onto the ground, and reveled in the feel of fresh air. The night air was filled with the smells of wildlife and the living. It occurred to him that he could just walk away right now. Leave the two opposing forces to battle it out, he didn't have to be there.

But as Drago sat up, and looked out over the sloping hills of the Carpathian Mountains, he saw Edward and his team blasting holes into the entrances of the cave. They were doing that to disarm the Carpathian women. Throw them all off balance enough so that they could enter and kill them all.

"Shit."

Drago got up and began heading down the hill towards Edward and his crew. He would negotiate a deal to save Cassandra's life at least. But the others could all burn as far as he was concerned.

He would try and talk some sense into Edward. As Drago made his way down the mountain, he made one stop by the plane that had belonged to his old friend, just as another blast broke through the hole in the tunnels.

***

Edward ordered another cannon fired into the ground, and watched as the rock formations was almost devasted enough for them to enter. He relished as he heard distant screams from below. Knowing the creatures were scampering like roaches. Good. He wanted them all dead. Every single one of them. And this time he would finish the job that should've been done long ago.

The men turned their guns as they saw someone come through the trees.

"Hold your fire men! It's one of ours."

Edward smirked as he saw Drago come trekking down the hill. He waited until he stood before him, and looked him up and down with a sneer.

"So, I see you finally decided to join us. Guess vampire pussy wasn't what you thought it was, huh?" Edward smiled viciously as he saw the heat and anger rise within Drago's eyes.

227

He chuckled and patted him on the shoulder.

"Stand down, Drago. You don't want to go toe to toe with me. I think you learned your lesson on that by now." Edward watched him with calculating eyes.

Drago held onto his fury with an iron fist. He said in a cool tone.

"Why didn't you get me out of that jail, Edward? I was in there for four years. You're part of the fucking government. I know you could've done something to free me. You let me rot in that cell for four damn years." Drago clenched his fists while he watched the man he loathed.

Edward cocked his head and shrugged, looking out over the progress of his men.

"You may not believe this, but I truly didn't know what happened to you. And even when I did, I couldn't afford to blow the cover of the agency. You knew the risks. It was a call I had to make."

Drago snorted and decided to lay the cards on the table.

"That's bullshit and you know it, Edward. All of this is nothing but a smoke screen for your obsession to prove that vampires exist.

You risked my life, and all the lives of these men and countless more. Just to satisfy your crazy ideals."

Drago could see the twitch begin to form over Edward's left eye. He pressed onward.

"The real reason you couldn't free me from that prison is because you knew the whistle would be blown. You knew the CIA would never back this ridiculous organization of yours, and that's why you had to get guys like me to do your dirty work for you. Guys you knew that if caught, would be blamed and labeled as terrorists because of my military background."

Drago faced him and looked him dead in the eyes. He'd changed his mind. He knew killing those women no matter what they were, was wrong.

"There's no reason to go through with this whole massacre, Edward. Doing this will prove absolutely nothing."

"Do you want to know why I chose you, Drago?"

Edward said calmly, as he continued to look out over his men, while they readied another cannonball.

"I chose you not because of your skills, although they did come in handy. I chose you, because I know you're weak."

Drago felt the rage rising within his chest, but kept a firm hand on his emotions. He balled up his fists, resisting the urge to flatten the self-absorbed psycho.

"You're a weak man, easily manipulated. And that is why you were perfect. Your brain skills weren't that impressive, so it fit my plan wonderfully." Edward turned now in satisfaction to look into Drago's eyes. A cold and gleaming expression resting within them.

"Did you really think I cared anything at all about your brother?" He chuckled and shook his head.

"I could care less about that skinny crack pipe fool. He was nothing but a means to an end. It was extremely easy, really. You see, I needed a reason to draw you into our organization. You were the main target, Drago. There is so much you don't know about all of this. And all the pieces that have been laid in place for this night to happen. For the destruction of the Carpathians."

Drago felt a cold chill race down his spine as he listened to what Edward was saying. Something heavy beginning to settle within the center of his chest.

"It goes back far beyond you and me. To the very beginning. The Carpathians thought they had us humans fooled. Thought they could hide their women somewhere, and that we wouldn't know about it? The fools! They were all stupid mindless animals and could never outsmart mankind. That's why they hid their females from us. But the secret organization that has lasted for centuries always knew they still existed. We bided our time. Handing down the legacy from generation to generation. Always searching, and waiting for the fools to make a mistake. And then they did."

Edward smiled wickedly, quite pleased with himself.

"Two centuries ago, their queen, Besilia was the whore's name, had this crazy idea that she would find a way to save her women. She ventured out by herself above ground, unbeknownst to the others, and mated with a human male. It was an attempt to see if Carpathians and humans could cohabitate together. She became pregnant instantly, and gave birth seven days later in the woods away from her home. The child died. At least, that's what she thought. She had buried the infant in the ground, and left. Returning to her people with a pledge that they would try to do what she couldn't.

The baby, you see was heard crying in the ground, by some hikers. They dug the child up and rescued him. Raised him as their own. But they found out soon enough, that he was not like any other child. He was a vampire. Part man and Carpathian. They gave the child up to an orphanage at the age of twelve, when the killings began."

Edward paused and stroked his beard in thought, as he watched Drago's face. Enjoying his confusion.

"The child was never seen or heard from again. He escaped the orphanage, and simply vanished. Until a few hundred years later, when it was reported that a woman had given birth to a baby with strange glowing eyes. She was a poor woman, who later had a second child by another man who abused her and eventually left her. But it was the first child she bore that the organization was interested in.

We had no proof, until one day it was reported that a hooded man came to visit her. He'd taken special interest in the boys, but especially the older son. He gave them both two Identical pendants. But it was the older child's eyes that glowed when he put it around his neck."

Edward looked at him and narrowed his eyes in victory.

"It was you, Drago. Your father was the halfling that had been born from the queen all those centuries ago. He'd remained hidden from us for so long, we weren't sure he even existed. But then, he fell for a human woman. It was always a woman." Edward laughed in delight.

"His fatal mistake was coming back to see you. We finally found him, tracked him to his lair. Even though he was a day walker, and wasn't affected by the sun, we still were able to end his miserable existence with a stake to the heart." He smiled in satisfaction.

"But I told the organization, that instead of killing you, let you live. Grow to a man. I knew you would one day lead us all the heart of the Carpathian people. All you needed was motivation. And your foolish brother provided that." He narrowed his eyes as he laid the final bomb, in the tunnel and in Drago's heart.

"We used your brother as bait for Cassandra. Made sure she would choose him for judgement. We placed him directly in her path, so that she would take him. She always teleported, so we could never track her. But thanks to you, we were able to finally pin her and the Carpathian people down.

Thanks to you...and your brother."

Chapter Twenty Five

Drago stood still as he was suddenly surrounded by three men pointing guns at his head. His eyes never left Edward, as all of the emotions swirled within him and was rising to the surface.

"I hope you don't take this personally, Drago. It was all a means to an end. The bug and tracker we planted in the plane, and Philip's untimely death by the Carpathians. It was all part of a grander design. My design. So you see, I would think again before labeling me as this deranged psycho. I'm the one that's still standing."

Drago gave a slow smile as he watched Edward, and casually glanced at the other men holding the guns at him.

"Are you certain of that, Edward? Do you really think you're the last one standing?"

Drago uttered the words just as a loud scream erupted within the air.

Edward turned with eyes wide, as he saw a group of Carpathians slicing through his men. The speed in which they came at them, made them appear as only a blur.

"Fall back! Fall back, men! They came out from another side!"

Edward reached for the special rifle, but Drago jammed his wrist swiftly within his neck, and caused him to stumble back, gasping and choking.

He snatched the rifle with amazing speed, and turned in the same breath, emitting the bright light within the faces of the men that surrounded him. They shot out blindly, as he stole one of their guns, and aimed three bullets to their heads. Taking them down instantly.

Drago turned in time to see Edward escaping into the hills, as his men were being slaughtered. Running like the coward he was.

He ran after him, following him up the cliffs and cornering him on the edge of the mountain.

Edward looked down in panic, knowing he was trapped. He turned around and saw Drago standing there, watching him, like predator to his prey.

"Did you really think you would get away with all of this, Edward?" Drago mocked him, using the same tone he had taunted him with earlier.

Edward's face was red with fury. He braced his legs apart, and smirked.

"I thought you were a soldier. Now you need women to fight for you? Really Drago? Let's see if you truly are a man, or nothing more than an abandoned abominable creature from hell."

Edward's words hit a nerve, and Drago lost it. He threw down the rifle, and charged at him.

Edward caught him with a powerful punch to the ribs, his fist encased around brass knuckles. Drago grunted in pain, as several of his ribs cracked on contact. But Edward continued to press his advantage while he had it.

He took his fist and slammed it directly into Drago's jaw with a blinding uppercut. Following it up with a blow to the head, and sending him spiraling to the ground as he jammed his brass knuckles into the left side of his ribs.

Drago fell to the ground, spitting and coughing blood from his mouth. The wound from his head starting to seep into his eyes and blur his vision.

Edward laughed uproariously, as he kicked him in the ribs again.

"You call yourself a man? You're not even a real vampire. You're just a halfling bitch like your father was. And your brother was our whore."

Drago shouted in rage and flew at him in a blinding speed.

Edward fell to the ground, as he cracked his fist across his face with such force, several of his teeth flew out in a bloody mess.

Drago was in a blinding heat of fury. His eyes began to glow and change color, they became a fiery red, and his teeth extended to sharp scissors.

Edward's eyes bulged in fear as he saw the evidence of the monster he'd spent his whole life chasing. Drago's face began to distort and grow into a grotesque mask of evil. A demon that wanted nothing but to feast and kill. His mouth opened wide as the saliva dripped into Edward's face.

"Now…. it's your turn to know what it's like to be afraid." Drago hissed and prepared to tear out his jugular.

"Drago…."

It was Cassandra. She was in his mind, inside his head. Like a cool balm to his seething heat. His hunger fought against her, demanding blood.

"Drago...no. His judgement is coming in another way. You know this already. Let him go. Don't lose yourself to the monster."

Cassandra reached out to him using the bond and connection they now shared. She poured herself into him, until the beast began to calm. It finally simmered down and evaporated. What replaced it was the presence of her essence. She gave him balance. Filled the void. She made him whole.

Drago threw Edward to the side, and fell to his knees, panting. His face and form changing back to his normal body once again. He looked at his hands and was left with so many questions. What was he? How could he live with himself, now that he knew the truth?

But even as he knelt on the ground, the loud approach of a helicopter interrupted his thoughts.

Edward stumbled to his knees as he saw that it was Bennet, and his men from the office. He quickly got to his feet, as Bennet jumped out with a few armed guards and rushed to his aide.

"Are you alright, sir?" Bennet asked Edward as the men, surrounded Drago with their guns.

Edward hid his smile of satisfaction, as he swiped the blood from his face, nodding his head. He looked back at Drago.

"This man tried to kill me and attacked my men with a group of his comrades. I want him detained immediately. He is the notoriously known escaped convict, and Russian spy. Take him away."

Edward smiled viciously at Drago.

"Of course sir, I would. Except for one thing. You see, a few hours ago, someone accessed a highly classified government issued tracking and bugging device from a plane, and fed it into the CIA frequency system. It allowed us to hear everything within a few miles' radius of the plane. So apparently, your plan to fraudulently use the government, and kill make believe creatures that you made everyone believe were simple telepaths, has now all been revealed."

Bennet broke out into a grin at the complete look of shock on Edward's bloody face. The armed guards lowered their guns towards Drago, and on Bennet's signal took Edward into custody, handcuffing his arms behind his back.

He turned and faced his old boss, and had a smug look in his eyes. It felt good to get back at the man that had destroyed his career.

"Now who's the fool, Beckman?" Bennet whispered to him, as he was carted away by the guards, while they read him his rights. Boarding him onto the helicopter.

Bennet turned towards Drago who had watched the whole thing in silence. A guarded look on his beaten and broken face.

He walked over to him and cleared his throat.

"I don't know exactly what happened out there tonight, but I want to thank you for opening our eyes to Edward's secret organization and activities. He's used me to do a lot of things for him, but I never knew it went this far."

He looked at Drago's face, and nodded.

"Edward will be blamed for the deaths of all those men out there. They shouldn't've been there. Now who and what they were fighting, I don't know, and don't want to. All I know is, their deaths are on Edward's hands. And you're free to go."

Drago looked at him and frowned.

"Yes, the government is exonerating you of all charges. You were under Edward's orders, and we heard what we he did to your family. That is something we can never give back to you. But at least, we can give you your freedom. Give you your name back."

Drago's jaw clenched as the pent up emotion boiled within him. No. He could never get any of it back. Not Philip. His brother. Or the father he never knew. But perhaps he could start changing things so that it could never happen to anyone else again.

Drago watched as Bennet got into the helicopter, and took off. The remaining silence was almost deafening. It took him a moment to realize that everyone else was gone. Turning back down the hill, he went back to scene of the battle. The gruesome showdown between man and Carpathian. It was a bloodbath. Only three Carpathian women were killed, he could see by the evidence of the glittering dust remains in several places. The rest were all human men. Torn bodies and ripped open flesh were everywhere. The mountainside that was normally so peaceful, was the scene of a small world war III.

"All of these lives. Wasted. Over what? When it will it all end?"

Drago said the words out loud, as he felt her approach. She was silent, yet a powerful force in his mind now. Everything now made sense.

Drago turned around and faced her. She was standing a few feet away from him. Her black thick curls were in a world of confusion around her face and shoulders. And she had replaced the white dress with her blue jeans and a black shirt. Both were bloodied, and tattered. Her face, a complete sculpture of untouched beauty surrounded by pain. Her green emerald eyes shining with the hint of tears.

They had both changed. Connected now in a way that could never be undone. Even if they wanted it to be.

He took a step towards her.

"So since you're fully in my mind now, I guess you can see the whole story that asshole Edward told me, huh?"

Cassandra took a step towards him and nodded her head silently.

"Yes. I can see everything. The moment you opened yourself up to the hunger, and almost turned full vampire, I saw you. I saw through your bloodline. The queen, and what she did, how she tried to save us by sacrificing herself. The birth of the halfling killed her, because she'd mated with a full human male. Their blood doesn't mix well with ours. But she'd done it to create your father. One whose blood would mix, and breed. But unfortunately, we never found him in time. She didn't die right away. But it had drained her too much. She did it for us. For her people. Edward was wrong. She knew the baby would live. That's why she buried it. That's why she tasked us to find the human man. One she knew would be part human, part Carpathian. A soul that would not be fully dark."

They were now standing directly in front of each other. He stared into her eyes. Eyes that saw so much. And smirked.

"I knew you were trouble from the first moment you walked towards me, looking like a delicious meal on a plate." He grabbed her body close, and breathed in the essence of her hair, her scent. Her light.

Cassandra sighed at the feel of his hardness once again. To be wrapped in his arms was all she'd wanted.

"That was just your hunger talking. The Carpathian in you that yearned to be set free."

She replied, as she lifted her head to his lips, his tongue feeling the texture and softness.

"So now what? Now that we know I'm part...Carpathian." Drago said softly into her lips, as he kissed her gently. Loving the way her body responded to him.

Cassandra moaned in satisfaction, as his hands wrapped around and gripped the shapely curves of her buttocks.

She smiled into his lips, and looked up into his now matching green emerald eyes. Eyes that glinted together with hers.

"That answer is easy. Now, we make lots of Carpathian babies together. And rebuild what was lost."

"Yeah...I like the sound of that."

Drago lifted her up in his arms and crushed her lips to his. The battle was momentarily forgotten, and so were all the dead bodies that surrounded them. Things were going to change for the better. And Drago and Cassandra would find a way for Carpathians and man to be at peace together, as they once were so long ago.

As the sun began to rise over the horizon, and touched both of their skin, neither of them noticed that Cassandra remained unscathed and unharmed by its powerful rays. Or the fact that a new life had already begun to form within her womb. A life that would be even more powerful, and bring about a change even quicker than they both realized.

Neither of them noticed. But they would be witness to a world that was about to change in more ways than one.

But for now.... the kiss that sealed their bond was the only difference that mattered in their existence of shadows and light.

And that was enough.

For now.

Epilogue

Edward Beckman Jr. sat in the interrogation room by himself. He'd been in there now for at least two hours, with no water, or appearance of any officers that were supposed to interview him regarding case files 501. Everything was unusually quiet, and the fact that no lawyer had showed up for him, did not look good at all.

Edward moved his stiff shoulders, and kept his handcuffed arms on the plain brown table. The hard chair was uncomfortable, but he ignored it, focusing his gaze on the glass window that lined one side of the wall. He knew they were watching him. Hoping the silence and long stretch of time would break him. But they would have to do better than that. He'd been in the game longer than most of them were alive. And he was seasoned. He knew the ropes. Edward was confident he'd find a way out of this. He always had an escape plan.

Suddenly, the door to the room opened up and a tall man walked in. He was very slim, with greying short hair and pale blue eyes. The man wore a plain navy blue business suit, and held a briefcase. He didn't say a word or introduce himself as he walked over and sat down at the table across from Edward.

Edward eyed the man questioningly and sat up with a smirk on his face.

"Well it's about damn time you showed up. I ordered a lawyer hours ago. I want out of these handcuffs, now. And I need to use my phone. I have someone I need to speak to immediately."

Edward made the demands and stared at the man, expecting his orders to be obeyed instantly.

But the gentleman never looked up at him. He simply placed his briefcase on the table, and opened it. Silently, he pulled out a silver cell phone and held it out to Edward. His gaze meeting his for the first time. The man's eyes were emotionless and empty.

Feeling the first prickle of unease, Edward frowned, staring at the phone in the man's hand.

"You have a phone call." The man said in a monotone voice.

Edward began to feel his heart quicken, but controlled his facial expression as he slowly took the phone from the stranger.

He remained calm as he placed the device to his ear. His eyes never leaving the man's face.

"Yes." Edward spoke into the phone.

There was an immediate reply.

"You've failed us, Edward. We are no longer in need of your services within our organization. Your membership is terminated."

Edward looked at the man in front of him, as he pulled out a silencer. And then stared at the glass window. They were watching him. Always watching.

The bullet hit dead center between his eyes. His body appearing shocked and surprised, before slowing crumpling forward onto the table.

The man silently replaced the gun into the briefcase and closed it. Leaving the table and exiting the room as silently as he had entered.

He walked to the three waiting agents that were standing behind the glass, observing the whole thing.

"It's done. Thank you for your service to the organization." The man shook all three CIA agent's hands, then killed them all. Aiming the bullet directly between their eyes at point blank.

"Thank you, but we don't like witnesses."

The man said calmly, and replaced the second gun he'd had on him back within his breast pocket. He removed the thin coat of plastic over his suit, designed to protect him from blood splatter. Retrieving his cell phone, he spoke into it clearly.

"It's done sir. All allies within this division have been sealed. They'd already agreed to remove all recording devices, so there's no evidence to lead back to us. It will all be blamed as an inside government corruption scandal. Our organization will not be touched."

The man nodded as he looked at the bodies, and the fallen figure within the interrogation room.

"Yes, sir. I followed protocol. Only the agents opened the door, and access points. My prints were left on nothing. The place is secure. I've already begun to look into phase two for you. You have my word on that."

The man placed the cell phone within his pocket and left the room using the access key from one of the agents. The door opened automatically. His fingers never had to touch a thing.

He walked out of the building making sure to keep his face averted from all outside cameras.

Now that all ties to the organization had been eliminated within the CIA, it was time to form new ones. And this time, they were going to start at the top.

The man stepped into his car, on his way to his appointment at the white house.

ABOUT THE AUTHOR

Born and raised in the Bronx. NY. Andrea Johnson was writing from the age of ten. She wrote and produced the first stage play in her junior high school, created paranormal short stories for her high school newspaper, and formed the youth group G.G.S. (God's Given Saints) at the age of twelve.

She is the CEO and President of a small marketing firm, co-owner of an insurance agency, and founder of Andrea Johnson Books Publishing. As well as the host of the electrifying web-series: Bedtime Mysteries. She directs and manages fundraising campaigns and community organizations of Christian developments, and female empowerment.

Her first book, Blood of my Blood, was released in 2009 and created inspiration to young new writers. Her stories have a reputation for the wild and unusual, and have been an entertainment for many years. Her motto is: Make each day count. And live every day as if it were your last. Andrea lives in Dallas TX with her family, her German Sheppard: Prince, and beautiful black cat: Rubia.

Visit Andrea's website to learn more about her upcoming books!

www.Andreajohnsonbooks.com

www.ingramcontent.com/pod-product-compliance
Lightning Source LLC
Chambersburg PA
CBHW030406020726
47493CB00003B/962